OTHER WORKS
BY BENJAMIN WALLACE

DUCK & COVER ADVENTURES
Post-Apocalyptic Nomadic Warriors (A Duck & Cover Adventure Book 1)
Knights of the Apocalypse (A Duck & Cover Adventure Book 2)
Last Band of the Apocalypse: A Duck & Cover Adventurette
Prisoner's Dilemma: A Duck & Cover Adventurette
How to Host an Intervention: A Duck & Cover Prequel
Gone to the Dogs: A Duck & Cover Prequel

BULLETPROOF ADVENTURES OF DAMIAN STOCKWELL
Horror in Honduras (The Bulletproof Adventures of Damian Stockwell)
Terrors of Tesla (The Bulletproof Adventures of Damian Stockwell)
The Mechanical Menace (The Bulletproof Adventures of Damian Stockwell)

DAD VERSUS
Dad Versus The Grocery Store
Dad Versus Halloween
Dad Versus Santa
Dad Versus The Tooth Fairy
Dad Versus Democracy
Dads Versus The World (Volume 1)
Dads Versus Zombies

OTHER BOOKS
Tortugas Rising

UNCIVIL
UnCivil: The Immortal Engine
UnCivil: Vanderbilt's Behemoth

SHORT STORIES
Alternate Realty
Dystopia Inc. #1: The War Room
Pilgrim (A Short Story)

Visit benjaminwallacebooks.com for more info.

BY

BENJAMIN WALLACE

ISBN-13: 978-1518685002
ISBN-10: 1518685005

This is a work of fiction. Names, characters, places, and incidents are the product of the author's imagination. Any resemblance to actual persons, living or dead, events, or locales is entirely.

Cover design by Monkey Paw Creative.

PRELUDE

SHIP OF HORROR

The room was filled with the kind of cold that would shake a man from his sleep and send him banging on the radiator while cursing the building's super. Kicking on the pipes wasn't an option. He wasn't in a building. And Gottfried von Brandt didn't sleep.

Von Brandt welcomed the cold in the ship's compartment. His lab coat and constant movement staved off chills, and he found it easier to stay focused when the room wasn't lulling him into comfort. There was no time to be comfortable.

A week had passed since he'd seen the sun. Ever since the ship left port. The makeshift laboratory space had met his needs perfectly in size and facilities and the lack of sunlight kept him focused on his work instead of the clock. The passage of time was a distraction he could do without, and had the compartment included portholes, he would have covered the glass to keep the sun outside where it belonged. He didn't need to think about time.

The scientist never left the compartment. There was no need. The ship's staff delivered his meals. These he ate only when he remembered to be hungry. Food didn't matter. Days didn't matter. Hours, minutes, nothing mattered but the deadline.

The World's Fair awaited him at the end of his voyage and he had to be ready. Time was the enemy and therefore best ignored. He didn't need to think about it. He needed to focus on how the machine should smile.

With one final twist he pulled a pair of pliers from the mouth of the device, stepped down from a small stool and backed away from the project that held his attention. He studied the face of the machine with the eye of an artist. He turned away and spun back quickly. The smile did not menace, smirk or show any signs of anything but pleasantry. It looked natural. He smiled back.

The machine itself was all but indistinguishable from a man. Perfect in size and proportion—Marie Tussaud would have commended the lifelike visage he had fabricated for the face. It was that of any man you would pass on the street. It was neither ugly nor handsome, but exquisitely average.

Looking into its eyes was a test of will and he soon felt overcome by the anxiousness that comes from staring and fearing being caught. The eyes were lifelike, but held no life. They were compassionate, but held no emotion. Gottfried had made them blue like his own, the one piece of a creator's vanity he had permitted himself. It was never intended to make him famous. It was built to save lives.

His machine wouldn't be the only one to debut at the Century of Progress exhibition. Others in the field of robotology had made breakthroughs that mirrored his own, and now they were all rushing to debut the man of tomorrow. The world would be watching, and they would all be clamoring for their share of the attention.

But his creation was different. He was different. Other robotologists labored in industrial labs filled with tools and equipment that were far beyond his facilities. They possessed a staff of scientists with the intelligence and degrees to accomplish the task but no passion. How could there be true passion when they worked for someone else? They were under contract to build the next great modern gadget. In a world of potential miracles they saw nothing but appliances to line department store floors. They were working on another Frigidaire. All they saw was a machine with a price tag.

While the others toiled to create servants and novelties to fill a housewife's wish list, he had greater ambitions. He was building a machine that would change the world.

He rolled up the robot's sleeve revealing a network of cables within a skeletal framework of steel so densely packed that they looked like muscle fibers. These worked in concert to multiply the machine's strength well beyond that of a normal man. While it had to look human, his machine could not be as weak as a man.

Von Brandt's creation was designed to blend in, look human and pass for normal right up until the moment it was needed. Once called upon to act, it would give selflessly of itself. A very inhuman trait. The machine would rush into danger—burning homes, collapsed buildings, traffic accidents—and save those in peril with no thought to its own well-being.

Gottfried gave it the strength to lift cars and rend iron. It couldn't burn, it couldn't suffocate, it could go anywhere and it would save anyone. With several of his machines in every city, he predicted accidental deaths would decline by as much as eighty percent. Policemen, firemen and hospital staff couldn't be everywhere. But his machine could.

Its usefulness didn't end in the streets. Mining. Logging. Construction. These perilous but necessary labors of man would also find a hero in his machine. Why send men into harm's way when a machine could assume the risk? And by removing men from the perilous jobs, even more lives would be saved.

He reached into the arm and plucked a cable at the elbow joint that looked suspect. To his satisfaction, the cord resonated with a high G. He withdrew his hand and wiped the elbow grease from his fingers onto his lab coat. The smear quickly blended with a patchwork of dirt and grime that had collected since his voyage began.

Von Brandt unrolled the sleeve and pulled it down to cover the exposed cabling. Once again, the machine looked just like a man. Gottfried stepped back and cocked his head as he studied the machine. He told himself it was finished, but he knew he would tinker and tweak everything until the minute they made port. Then he would tweak it some more again on the train to Chicago. But for the moment, he was done. He would power it up in the morning and put it through its paces again and again.

He told himself he was finished for now and that he could sleep. He had earned some rest. If not for the gift he was about to give the world, simply for the labor he had put into trying. A yawn overtook him and he stretched his arms out full. Yes, some rest would do him good.

He cast one last glance at his machine. That smile was perfect. Just enough humanity. Just enough confidence. But not too much of either to intimidate or frighten. It was a fine line between putting someone at ease and making their spine crawl. He had found that line. The smile was perfect.

Von Brandt smiled back one more time.

Then the machine moved.

1

Morning of the Machine

"Like a pancake?" Bertrand sat behind the wheel of the Pierce-Arrow limousine with impeccable posture. The chauffeur's cap on his head barely moved as he spoke over his shoulder to the man behind the newspaper in the rear seat of the elegant car. The cap sat, as always, at a proper angle.

"That's what it says in the *Tribune*, my French ami," the man said as he folded the paper. His presence filled the rear seat of the limousine. At six foot four inches, Damian Stockwell towered over the smallest of men and rose slightly above taller ones. "They found him flattened like a pancake."

"I don't understand zis espression."

"It would be like a quiche to you. A really flat breakfast dish," Stockwell said. "Very delicious."

"Oh, zat ees une crepe," Bertrand said.

"No, it is not crap. It says so right here in the World's

Greatest Newspaper. And I will not have you questioning the integrity of our country's journalists."

"Non," Bertrand shook his head slightly. "I meant zee pancake ees like une crepe."

"Watch your language, Bertrand. There's a lady present." Damian shot a smile to the woman across from him and allowed a single twinkle to bounce off his eye. They were the blue of silver coin in the moonlight and silver like the bluest oceans, and experience had taught him that more than one twinkle could be too much. "Isn't that right, Ms. Palmer?"

He could tell that she didn't know how to respond. He often had this effect on women. Normally they would get flustered. Often they would blush. They'd look away and then back and away once more before falling into his eyes. But not Angelica Palmer.

The woman sat there in her journalist's suit, her rich auburn hair falling like sunset from beneath her journalist's hat while she scratched in her journalist's notebook, which sat neatly on her journalist's lap, all the while holding a very journalistic look on her face. This woman was all business. Her business was journalism.

Angelica Palmer cleared her throat and sat up a little straighter. "Mr. Stockwell—"

"Please, Angelica. You've been traveling with me for how long now?"

"Five weeks," she said with professional accuracy.

"Five weeks," he repeated as if she hadn't said it. "In that time you've seen me in business meetings at my most cunning. You've seen me at charity events at my most compassionate. You remember the orphanage?"

"I do."

"You've even seen me cry." Damian looked out the window for a brief moment and watched the electric lights of Chicago roll by. "When I cut that onion while making dinner, so you've seen me at my most culinary. If anyone has earned the right to forgo formalities, it's you. Call me Damian. Or Dam."

"Well, I really don't see why I should start now, Mr. Stockwell. After the unveiling tonight, I'll have to leave you and write my story."

"And I'll be the first to read it."

He loved the way she smiled when she didn't mean it, because deep down he knew she did. She did this now and said, "You flatter me."

"No, I'll be the first. My lawyers insisted." He smiled and meant it.

She tilted the brim of her hat a little lower.

"I can see you're not in the mood for jokes, Ms. Palmer. Maybe we should go back to what you're most comfortable with. Do you have any questions for me?"

"How does that story in the paper make you feel?"

Damian Stockwell, great adventurer, captain of industry and paragon of right, rolled his eyes. "Really? Again with the feelings?"

"It's an interesting development in the story. I think my readers would be interested in your reaction."

Stockwell pointed to the paper. "How is this about me?"

"The man was one of your major competitors, was he not? He was set to debut at the exposition, but instead he arrives dead in New York, seemingly killed by his own creation. How does that make you feel?"

"How do you think it makes me feel, Angelica? It makes me sad. Gottfried von Brandt was one of the world's foremost robotologists. His work was remarkable. And now he's dead. Death is never a welcome change. It comes wrapped in regret with the cold fingers of emptiness reaching into the hearts of everyone that knew him. For those that knew him well there is an aching that will never heal. For those that knew him less, there is the remorse of not knowing him more. The brilliance of his genius was snuffed out long before it could illuminate the world." Stockwell leaned forward and looked her in the eye. "How could I feel anything but a great sadness for these events? And you can print that."

"He said your work was irresponsible and self-serving."

"Well, then I'm less sad than I normally would be." Damian leaned back in his seat. "But still sad, nonetheless."

"You aren't the least bit relieved that your competition is out of the way?"

"Iron sharpens iron, Ms. Palmer. One man sharpens another. Both the Bible and iron workers taught us this. Not only do I welcome competition, I crave it. Competition is what makes both man and our country great. And you can print that."

Angelica tapped the pencil against her notebook. "Are robots dangerous?"

"You've asked me this before."

"I'm asking you again."

"What makes you think my answer has changed?"

"The man was flattened like a pancake."

"Robotology is a young science. And any science brings danger. When you stick your fingers into the unknown you're hoping to find miracles, but you risk sticking those fingers into peril. Should we withdraw our fingers and continue living with our own stupidity? No. We face these dangers head-on with our chin up, chest out and our fists set like steel. It is our job as scientists to conquer that danger and wrestle it to our will. Only then will we progress beyond the hell of our own ignorance. And you can print that. Except for the swearing. I don't think they'll let you print that."

"Many fear that robots will turn on us. And several prominent robotologists have been mysteriously killed in the last several months, seemingly proving that point."

"We've designed these machines to be like friends to us. Loyal, selfless, dedicated. We've made them as human as possible. Of course they'll turn on us. It's inevitable."

"How do you plan to handle that?"

"With very good lawyers." Stockwell smiled at his own joke, knowing full well it wasn't really a joke at all.

Angelica did not return the smile. "How about just not

making robots?"

Stockwell shrugged. "You can't stop progress." He turned away and looked out the window. The Pierce-Arrow rolled slowly through a throng of people as it pulled up to the home-builders' showcase in the Century of Progress Exhibition. The crowd was courteous enough to step aside but rushed the windows of the limousine. They pressed their faces against the glass to get a better look at the man inside.

Damian's adventures were widely published in newspapers around the world and few had not heard of the Guardian of Good. The public felt as if they knew him intimately from newsreels and radio, but to actually see the man in person was something they could forever hold over their friends.

Damian smiled at each man, woman and child that braved the running board.

The car slowed to a stop in front of the DamIndustries home of tomorrow. The home was built with clean lines, composite materials, plastic windows and an artificial lawn that required zero maintenance and was only suspected of being slightly toxic to small pets and children.

Bertrand set the parking brake and killed the engine. "We have arrived, Monsieur."

"Look out there," Stockwell said in a hushed voice. "You can't really see it because of all the faces against the window, but behind that crowd of ravenous fans sits a house from the future. Every amenity. Every luxury. Every comfort. And even though everyone will be able to afford it, it's a home fit for the President of the United States of Tomorrow. And you can print that."

"Why, thank you," she said with little appreciation.

Stockwell's smile briefly faded. "Bertrand."

"Oui, Monsieur?"

"This self-opening door isn't going to open itself now, is it?"

"Non, Monsieur."

The roar of the crowd filled the car as the valet opened the driver door and made his way to the passenger compartment. He cleared the crowd back from the limo and pressed a button on the car. The limousine door flew open for Damian, and the world embraced him.

The giant man stepped from the car and waved to the people before him as security parted the crowd. They cheered him on as the press rushed into the void, popping, ejecting and reloading flashbulbs as fast as their fingers permitted. The ground quickly became covered with broken glass and crunched like snow beneath their feet as they tried to outmaneuver one another for the perfect shot.

Stockwell was accustomed to the attention and took it all in stride. He called to a few familiar faces. "Jimmy, good to see you. Carl, how are the kids? Still working for that yellow rag, Danny?" He shook hands and moved through the host of journalists, passing each one off to his side. Before they knew it they were between their subject and the car.

They weren't interested in his questions. The reporters broke past the line of photographers and rushed up to him, each vying for the first question. They shouted their names and the names of their papers, but, in the end, they were all asking the same question.

"Are the rumors true, Mr. Stockwell?"

"People are talking, Mr. Stockwell, give our readers the truth."

"Do you care to comment on the rumors, Mr. Stockwell?"

"How long have you been seeing one another?"

"Does it tickle?"

Stockwell raised his hands above the crowd and it fell silent. "Now, everyone please settle down. As you know, tonight is a big night for DamIndustries, and for the world. We're about to make history and give humanity a gift of freedom like it's never known. I know we've been secretive about our project, and I thank you for your patience. All will be revealed in a matter of time. With that said, I will answer one question now. So, what's it going to be?"

One hand went up faster than the others, and Stockwell pointed to the reporter leaning against the car.

Ted Starr had a face made for slapping. Add in his cocksure smile and you'd be willing to turn that slap into a punch. Called upon, he turned up the smile and spoke. "Ted Starr, *Evening Herald*. Rumor has it that you and one of the stars of the fair are an item. Do you care to comment?"

Damian smiled broadly and nodded. "It's true."

The crowd gasped and then giggled.

Stockwell pointed north up the fairgrounds toward two massive steel towers. They rose over two hundred feet into the air and peaked with observation decks. They sat nearly two thousand feet apart with the harbor between them. Several rocket-shaped passenger cars traversed the distance on high tensile cables, emitting a blast of red rocket steam as they went. "The Sky Ride and I have been seeing each other for a little over a month."

The crowd laughed as crowds do when they are being polite.

Ted Starr was not amused. "I'm referring to the rumors that you've been receiving private fan dance lessons after hours."

"I'm sure I don't know what you're talking about, Mr. Starr, but I would refrain from making any assumptions that could put your paper at risk." Stockwell turned to the crowd. "Now, if you'll excuse me, everyone. The future awaits!"

The reporters were trained to stay in front of their subject until they got the story. They learned early on to persist until the byline was written. For most, this doggedness was in their very nature and they found themselves comfortable forming a barricade of questions against the unwilling. But, as Stockwell stepped forward, they moved aside. They knew too well that he had said all that he was going to say. Standing in his way would only result in what they came to call the Stockwell Treatment, which only led to humiliation and capitulation.

Angelica followed close behind him, nodding to a few of her colleagues as she passed.

"Hey, Palmer," Starr called out from against the car.

His call turned the woman and Stockwell back to the reporter.

Starr lit a cigarette and waved out the match. "How'd you get this story? Do you know something about fans?"

Angelica snapped the pencil in her hand and moved towards Starr.

Stockwell narrowed his eyes on the cavalier reporter. He had no tolerance for rudeness. There was never an excuse for it, and it upset his chivalry when it was directed towards a lady. He felt his fists get angry and the crowd grow nervous. "Bertrand."

The valet stood next to the reporter at the rear of the limo. "Oui, Monsieur?"

"The door felt like it was sticking."

Bertrand pressed the release button on the side of the Pierce-Arrow and the passenger door flew open, striking Starr in the back of the head before sending him to the concrete.

"It's seem fine now, Monsieur."

"Hmmm. That it does. Thank you for checking, Bertrand. Leave the car. We'll move it later."

The valet doffed his hat, closed the door and stepped over Starr. He made his way through the crowd of reporters as they laughed at the man on the ground.

Angelica Palmer wasn't pleased. She crossed her arms beneath a scowl. "I can handle myself, Mr. Stockwell."

"Forgive me, Ms. Palmer. I have no doubt you can handle yourself, but I'm a gentleman and I wanted to handle you for you." He smiled at her once more. "And please call me Dam."

Bertrand jogged to catch up to the pair, his hat never shifting out of place.

Angelica waited for him. "Thank you for that, Bertrand."

"My pleasure, Mademoiselle."

"Tell me, Bertrand. What do you think of robots?"

Bertrand smiled. "I sink zey are a wonderful idea."

2

Je, Robot

When a man is forced to face himself—in instances of quiet reflection or those desperate moments when faced with his own mortality—he finally knows who he is. He learns, in that moment of epiphany, what he is capable of. His flaws are exposed, his weaknesses are laid bare, but his virtues rise through the vices and he knows his true worth. As Bertrand came face-to-face with himself, he only had one thing to say. "Zis eez a terrible idea!"

The valet stood in the middle of the stage looking into his own eyes. The machine was nothing like he imagined. When Stockwell had told him about the robotic personal assistant, the valet had imagined the machine with a featureless face of brushed metal on a skeletal frame with enough arms to manage the chores of the demanding elite as if it had leapt from the garish covers of the rags at the newspaper stand.

"What's the matter, Bertrand?" Stockwell asked from across

the room. "You look shocked."

The valet pointed at the machine in front of him. "Zis ees me!"

Stockwell laughed and excused himself from a conversation he'd been engaged in with a man in a lab coat. The titan crossed the stage with relatively few steps and put his hand on the robot's shoulder. "It sure is. Do you like it?"

Bertrand looked at himself closer. The skin was Bakelite or ceramic or something else entirely and not the most detailed, but there was no mistaking his own features. His eyes, his hair, his nose—even the sign of the break he had suffered long ago on the docks of Marseille—it was indeed his own face. The valet winced in disgust. "Non!"

Damian took a step back. His eyebrows pinched and peaked above the pools of blue and silver. "I thought you'd be flattered."

"Zis ees un insult!"

"How is it an insult? This, my friend, is a compliment of the highest order. This machine will be the desire of women everywhere. There isn't a housewife in the country that won't want to get her hands on it. It will make all her wishes come true. I just made you the most desirable man in America, Bertrand."

The robot was dressed in the traditional, formal style of the valet. A finely woven morning jacket hung over a silk vest and accented by a matching pocket square and cravat. Bertrand had a similar outfit hanging in his wardrobe. He reached out and touched the collar and felt a familiar fray hidden behind the lapel. "Zeese are my clozes on a ... on a toaster!"

Stockwell stepped from behind the other Bertrand and placed his hand on the real Bertrand's shoulder. "My friend, my dear and loyal companion. We've been on many great adventures together, have we not? I'm not trying to sell the world an appliance. I'm trying to give the world the gift of companionship that you have given me. This is my way of paying forward the generosity, the faithfulness and the laundry folding that you have shown me all these years. Why should I be so blessed when the rest of the world must go without? Just because I'm fabulously wealthy? That hardly seems fair."

Bertrand felt a stir inside that tried to crawl out his eye. Being a personal valet to a man such as Damian Stockwell had not been without its perils and irritants. The man lived an unparalleled life of daring and adventure. Oftentimes the dangers of such a life came with such incessant abandon that Stockwell took little time to reflect on anything but the threat of the moment.

Damian moved beside the new Bertrand. "No, my dear Bertrand. The whole world deserves a friend like you." He straightened the lapel on the morning jacket and backed away. "Exactly like you."

"Besides," the man in the lab coat spoke as he joined the pair before the robot. The words still held the cadence of a German accent, but his pronunciation was precise. "We wanted to give it some personality. But we had to start with a simple one."

Stockwell smiled and made the introductions. "Bertrand, this is Doctor von Kempelen, DamIndustries' head robotologist."

The doctor stuck out his hand and smiled. "It truly is an honor to meet you, Bertie."

The valet took the hand because it was polite, but he looked at Stockwell for further explanation. "What ees zis Bertie?"

"My apologies, Bertrand," the doctor said. "I feel as if I know you so well. I've spent months inlaying you into the Val-8 … I've come to think of you as a friend. And as a friend I gave you a nickname—Bertie."

"Inlaying me?"

"It's not as gross as it sounds, Bertrand," Stockwell said. "I checked."

"Yes, inlaying you. I taught the Val-8 all about you. Your mannerisms, your speech patterns … Would you do me a small favor? Would you please say for me, 'Would you like to lick the spoon'?" The robotologist smiled.

Stockwell hid a laugh behind his hand.

"Non, I don't want to do zat."

"Oh, please. It's my favorite."

"Non."

"Bertrand, why are you being so difficult?" Stockwell reached to the back of the robot's neck.

There was a click and a whir and a kachunk that would have to be checked before the unveiling. The hum of warming tubes finished off the chorus.

Stockwell looked the Val-8 in the eyes and spoke. "Bake me a cake, Val-8."

"Oui. Would you like to leak ze spun?"

Damian had a glorious laugh that could, and had, turned the fortunes of men and women around the world. The doctor's was more a schoolgirl giggle and hurt a little less.

Bertrand pointed a wagging finger at the machine. "I do not zound like zat."

"Oh, please," Stockwell said. "Everyone says that when they hear themselves."

"It sounds exactly like him." Angelica had stood in awe of the machine while the valet protested.

"That's because it's his voice." Stockwell pulled a small device from his pocket. "I've been secretly recording him for months."

"Zut alors! You've been secretly … How could you?"

"How could I not, Bertrand?" Stockwell said as he put the device away. "We needed the Val-8 to sound natural, not like some amateur French version of Hamlet."

"How can you do zis wisout telling me?"

"That's what secretly means, Bertrand."

"I have never—"

"Relax, it's not like you weren't compensated."

"You have given me nothing for zis."

"Do you remember when you asked for last Thursday off?"

Bertrand's eyes darted to the ceiling and back. "Oui."

"And did I say anything?"

"Non."

"Well there you have it."

Bertrand prided himself on his complete self-control, but he felt the heat rushing to his face and embraced the rage. He tried to say something hurtful, but it escaped his lips in such a rush of French that even Napoleon would have to ask, "Pardon et moi?" He gasped and switched to English. "You are incredible."

Damian smiled. "That's what the papers say."

The valet turned on his heel and stomped off. "I'm going to park ze car."

"It was nice to meet you, Bertie," the doctor said.

Angelica watched the man from Marseilles storm away. "Is he going to be okay?"

"He'll be fine," Stockwell assured her and turned to the scientist. "But, while Bertrand is sulking, we should take this opportunity to put the Val-8 through its paces."

"The Val-8?" She had her notebook in hand. She was all reporter once more.

"It stands for Valet Eight," Stockwell explained. "But we call it The Bertrand. Bertrand may be pouty, but everyone deserves someone as efficient as him in their lives."

"But why eight?" she asked.

Johan von Kempelen shrank into his lab coat as he answered loud enough for her to hear but soft enough that he hoped she wouldn't. "The Val-7 had a cat murdering problem."

"Did you say cat murdering?"

Stockwell shrugged. "It saw them as pests. Who could blame it?"

"But we've fixed that, and the cats are safe. Just watch what it can do." Von Kempelen turned the Val-8 back on.

The machine hummed and its mouth opened like a marionette's. "Bonjour. 'ow may I be of zervice?"

"Val-8, I'm a little hungry. How about a sandwich?"

"Oui, Monsieur." The Val-8 looked at the three people before him.

"Right now, it is calculating the best path to the kitchen. His sensors detect all living things and he plans a route around them."

"Even cats, now," Stockwell added.

The Val-8 turned left and stepped toward the kitchen. Despite its construction, it didn't lumber or stomp. It stepped gently and discreetly, so as not to disturb anyone unjustly. It stepped just like Bertrand.

Damian, the doctor and the reporter followed the machine as it moved through the model home into the kitchen and set about its task.

It opened the fridge, located a ham and turned it over several times.

The robotologist narrated the Val-8's motions. "Right now it is calculating the condition of the meat. It can detect multiple toxins, bacteria and more. Food poisoning and icky ham hands will be a thing of the past."

The Val-8 set the ham on a cutting board and sliced several pieces before returning the meat to the fridge. It located a loaf of bread in the pantry and repeated the inspection and cutting process. Within moments, the sandwich was dressed, plated and held before them.

Stockwell raised the sandwich and took a massive bite.

"That's incredible," Angelica said. "What else can it do?"

Damian nodded and looked at the Val-8. He spoke with a mouth full of sandwich, "Vrmph eicht, mean mif phwace sup."

Von Kempelen smiled. "Right now it is calculating what exactly Mr. Stockwell said and determining how such a renowned man could be so successful with such poor manners."

Angelica chuckled.

"Mwat?" asked Stockwell.

The doctor spoke to the robot. "Val-8, clean this place up."

What followed this command was nothing short of a leap into the future. The Val-8 surveyed the showroom. It was spotless. A staff of designers had planned, cleaned and laid out the room for the perfect presentation. Nothing was out of place. Still, the Val-8 set about the room correcting the position of items: straightening pictures, adjusting chairs, organizing the spice rack according to most common usage as opposed to alphabetical as the design team had.

Within minutes the kitchen was more perfect than perfect, and the Val-8 left the room.

The group followed the machine as it moved about the model home making slight adjustments before coming to rest back in the middle of the living room where it all began.

The group turned as Bertrand returned through the front door of the model home. "You are all still fawning over zat contraption?"

Stockwell spoke again to the machine. "Val-8, please console Bertrand."

The Val-8 moved without hesitation towards the valet.

Bertrand took a step back as it approached. "What ees zis?"

The machine stood next to the Frenchman, stuck out an arm and began to pat him slowly on the back.

Bertrand swore at it and tried to move away, but it followed him about the room, always patting him.

"This thing is amazing." Angelica scratched another note in her journal as she asked, "Is there anything it can't do?"

"The dishes," said von Kempelen.

"And I still wouldn't trust it with cats," said Stockwell. "Just to be safe."

"It can't do the dishes?" the reporter asked.

"Unfortunately, no," said the doctor. "We are still perfecting the waterproofing, but its internal machinations are just too sensitive to water."

"That's a pretty big drawback," she said. "Don't you see that as a significant shortcoming?"

Stockwell answered the question. "We believe that our Synthetic Intelligence will distinguish the Val-8. While its appearance is not, by design, truly human, our protocols make living with the Val-8 nearly indistinguishable from having another Bertrand in your home."

"Doctor," Angelica asked. "What do you think of the death of Gottfried von Brandt?"

"It's truly a tragedy. I knew Gottfried well. To expire in such a silly accident."

"Some people think that it was his machine that killed him."

"We scientists pursue the mysteries of the universe at our own peril, Ms. Palmer. On this adventure we hope to better understand our world so that we may better serve mankind. But it doesn't matter which field we choose to serve: physics, chemistry, lepidoptery or robotology. There is always a risk that nature is not ready to reveal herself to us, and she very well may kill us to keep her secrets."

"I never realized science was so scary," Angelica said.

"The idea is nothing new, of course. Mary Shelley wrote about it more than a century ago. When the doctor in her book faces his retribution at the hands of his own creation—it's a fable of sorts for scientists and, as with all fables, we take from it a moral that guides our work. Now if you'll excuse me, I must go prepare for the Val-8's debut."

The reporter stopped him as he walked away and asked, "What is that moral, Doctor?"

"Don't make anything too deadly."

3

Presentation of Peril

The DamIndustries home of tomorrow was full of wonders, electrified and otherwise. There was an appliance for everything. Designed and labeled under DamIndustries Ingenious brand, there wasn't a modern problem, real or perceived, that a DamIng appliance could not solve once plugged into the wall. Juicers, cleaners, air treatment processors, automatic pet doors and pet patters shined with polished perfection, inviting the housewife of today to think of DamIng for her home tomorrow.

But DamIng's innovations didn't just plug into the wall. DamIng's asbestos line was leading the way in innovation. Fireproof and energy efficient, the magical material had found its way into the flooring, walls and attic—the modern miracle was placed everywhere to make the home a safer place.

The DamIndustries house was one of a dozen "Homes of Tomorrow" in the Home and Industrial Group Area. Other companies had constructed their vision of the future here as well. One home was built of enamel, another steel. One manufacturer had developed glass blocks so you could feel like you were outside when you were actually inside. Or vice versa. All in all the manufacturers had envisioned a glorious future and brought it here to the pavilion.

And then there was the Dahlia Society. They just brought flowers.

Stockwell had nothing against flowers. And he hoped the future would have flowers. But the space occupied by the Dahlia Society was room that could be used to explore the incredible possibility of man's existence beyond today. But no, they planted flowers, and now that future would have to wait all because of the Dahlia Society.

"This place is amazing." Angelica strolled around the room. "It's so quiet in here."

"The insulation is designed to keep tempered air in and the sound of your neighbors out. Now you don't even have to learn their names well enough to tell them to keep it down," Damian explained. "Look outside. You'll see how well it works."

"You've got quite a crowd out there." Angelica peered through the automatic asbestos Venetian blinds at the audience gathered in the pavilion as Stockwell and von Kempelen made final preparations to the Val-8. "You're never going to fit them in here."

Damian Stockwell smiled. "Ha, of course not. Are we ready, Doctor?" Damian crossed the room to the portrait that hung on the wall. He pulled at the corner of the frame. It swung open, revealing an electrical panel too elaborate to simply be the home's fuse box.

Doctor von Kempelen lowered a sheet over the Val-8. "We are ready, Mr. Stockwell."

"Then it's time to start the show." Stockwell threw an electrical switch. Sparks flew from the contacts as the circuit closed. The furniture in the living room began to displace, sliding out of the way as a rumble built beneath the floor.

Angelica struggled to find her balance as the ground beneath her began to move. "What's going on?"

"Sacre bleu!" Ever the gentleman, Bertrand rushed to her side to catch her should she fall.

"You two should have a seat," Damian said.

"What is this?" Angelica let Bertrand guide her to a sofa that had snuck up behind them. The pair sat as the couch slid in front of a demonstration platform that rose out of the ground.

"It's a convertible." Stockwell closed the portrait and backed out of the living room as the front of the house swung open to thunderous applause.

Spotlights boomed to life and cut rays of brilliance through the night. A bandstand emerged from the floor with what appeared to be a relieved and slightly claustrophobic ensemble in place. They took a few deep breaths before striking into song.

The crowd outside grew exponentially as the home transformed itself into a stage. Fairgoers rushed to find the source of the lights, the music, the oohs and the ahhs. They weren't disappointed. Fireworks erupted from the corners of the stage as a chorus line of dancers filed in from each side of the home. Fifty girls dressed in red tights lined with sequins high-kicked as they made their way across the stage.

Angelica pulled Bertrand back into the couch as a glittery shoe breezed by his face.

"Thank you, Mademoiselle. I was distracted by zee lights."

"Uhh huh," Angelica dropped back into the couch and uncrossed her arms only to make a notation in her notebook.

The dance continued for two more numbers ensuring that the majority of the fair's visitors had gathered in the home's courtyard.

"He sure knows how to draw a crowd, doesn't he?" Angelica asked.

"Oui, Mademoiselle. He does indeed."

The band stopped, the crowd quieted and Damian's voice boomed all around them. "Ladies, gentlemen, children, my fellow citizens of today ..." The dancers lined up on either side of the

stage revealing Stockwell at its center. The microphone in his hand
delivered his voice across the Home and Industrial Group Pavilion
and beyond. "I'd like to welcome you to the DamIndustries home
of tomorrow and thank you for joining us tonight. Today we take a
giant leap from yesterday into the future."

Fireworks erupted again and the crowd roared.

"I've seen it, and I invite you to come with me now into a
world of convenience and comfort. In this world there are no
longer menial tasks to distract us from the important pursuits of
man: reading, writing, sporting and exploring. With the latest
DamIndustries breakthrough, we will finally be free to chase the
dreams of our forefathers and their forefathers before them."

Angelica placed her face in her hand and shook her head.

"Ladies and gentlemen, I'd like to take this opportunity to
invite to the stage a man that I believe possesses the best qualities
of humanity. Many of you have read of my adventures around the
world. What you might not know is that one thing they have in
common—aside from being incredibly amazing, frighteningly
dangerous, fraught with peril, spectacularly heroic and completely
selfless—is that on each and every one of some of them, I did not
go alone. No, even the world's greatest adventurer needs help from
time to time.

"I'd like to introduce you to Bertrand, my loyal valet and
dear friend."

The crowd applauded.

"Bertrand, come on up here."

The Frenchman shook his head and refused to move.

"He's a little shy, folks. Maybe we could encourage him."

The crowd slowly began to chant Bertrand's name, but due
to some confusion that began in the back of the crowd, they
chanted "Dan" instead. The chant grew until the valet finally rose
and stepped onto the stage. He stood next to Stockwell and bowed
his head to the crowd.

"Here he is, everyone, my dear friend and constant
companion, Bertrand. If not for him, I can surely say that I would

not be standing before you today. He has traveled with me into the face of danger and down to the depths of terror. He has saved my life on countless occasions and provided assistance in every one of my great achievements. He is a gift to the world and it would be selfish of me to keep him to myself. No, ladies and gentlemen, everyone deserves a Bertrand in their lives. This man right here was our inspiration for what you are about to see."

Stockwell smiled at his good friend before turning back to the crowd.

"Come with me now into tomorrow as I introduce to you the DamIndustries Val-8 personal assistant." Damian stepped away from the shrouded machine as the drape rose, the band began to play and fireworks lit up the sky.

The crowd gasped as the machine was slowly revealed. There was a hush of awe once the drape was clear. The hush of awe turned into a confused silence.

"It's just a guy," some guy in the audience said.

"Yeah," a thick Brooklyn accent joined in. "An ugly guy."

"I assure you, the Val-8 is no guy," Damian's voice boomed over the loud speaker. "It is a highly sophisticated personal assistant. Or, as we like to call it, The Bertrand. The Val-8 is the future."

Fireworks erupted and Stockwell rethought his plan to tie the explosions to the mention of the word future.

Damian continued. "The Val-8 is the ultimate in home automatonamation. The leading edge in robotology."

"Oh, it's a robot," the guy in the crowd said.

"It's not just a robot. The Val-8 is your personal butler, housekeeper and cook. It does everything you never wanted to do for yourself. It will tend your home, prepare your meals and handle your affairs."

Brooklyn spoke up once more. "I kind of like handling my own affairs."

"Why don't you say something, Bertrand?" Stockwell asked.

Bertrand reached for the microphone.

Damian pulled it away. "Sorry, I meant the other Bertrand."

This delighted the crowd and several pointed to Bertrand as they laughed.

The Val-8 raised its arm and the crowd gasped. It tipped its hat and spoke a tiny impression of Bertrand's accented English. "Bonjour."

The crowd gathered in the Home and Industrial Group Area erupted in applause.

Stockwell smiled and let it roll over him. He leaned over to Bertrand and spoke over the crowd. "If they think the hat thing is great, wait till they can see what else it does."

"I cannot believe you called it ze Bertrand," the Frenchman whispered with no concern for volume.

Damian flinched. "I thought you'd like it."

"Non."

"It's flattering."

"Stop saying ees flattering. Eet ees not flattering!"

Damian put an arm around Bertrand's shoulder and waved to the audience. "Just calm down, my friend. We don't want you to blow a croissant."

"What does it do?" The voice came from a blue-haired old woman in the front row. Security had brought her a chair and she sat with both hands folded over her purse. She leaned forward when she spoke and it was not without great effort.

"I'm so glad you asked, my dear lady. But it may be easier to ask what doesn't it do?"

The old woman wheezed as she sighed. "Fine. What doesn't it do?"

Stockwell stammered. "No, let's go back to your first question. The Bertrand ..." Stockwell looked at his valet and moved him aside so he could be standing next to the Val-8 as he spoke. "The Bertrand is nothing short of a modern miracle of science and engineering. This mechanical man will make your life a dream. It will clean your house: dusting, vacuuming, sweeping, rug beating are all things of the past. It will tend to your guests:

answer the door, escort them in and," Stockwell pulled a cigar from his pocket.

The Bertrand raised an outstretched hand and clicked. A flame ignited and burned at the end of The Bertrand's thumb.

Damian puffed it to life before continuing. "It cleans. It cooks. It folds. It fluffs. It dusts. It's the perfect gentleman housekeeper."

"Does it do the dishes?" asked the old woman.

Stockwell smiled. "I'm sorry. We already answered your question. Let's give someone else a chance."

"Does it do the dishes?" Ted Starr had a welt on his forehead and a grin on his face better suited for a matinee villain.

"The Bertrand is a modern miracle. And as we all know, miracles should not get wet. Next question."

"Will it murder me?" the blue-haired woman asked.

"Not from you, sweetheart. A question from someone else."

"It seems like a fair question in light of recent events. Will it murder her?" Starr asked.

"Of course not," Stockwell said.

"But the one robot killed that man in the papers," said the old woman.

Doctor von Kempelen stepped forward and leaned in towards the microphone. "The fact is we don't know what happened to Doctor von Brandt. He was a colleague of mine, and those of us in the robotologist community will mourn his loss. But, until we know what happened, it would be wise to assume it was an accident."

"So I can write down accidental murderous robot?" Starr asked with his pencil in the air.

"Regardless of whatever happened to my friend, The Bertrand has been designed with multiple safeguards that would prevent it from hurting anyone."

"Unless you're a cat," Damian added.

Doctor von Kempelen sighed and looked away.

"Or a puppy that looks a lot like a cat."

The doctor addressed the old woman again. "The Val-8 model is safe, my dear. It is designed only to serve you." The doctor turned to Stockwell, covered the microphone and asked a question.

Damian smiled and nodded.

Von Kempelen spoke in the mic again. "Why don't you join us on stage and we'll show you exactly how easy this machine is to use."

Stockwell began the applause and it rippled through the crowd until the old woman rose to her feet. The applause grew as she made her way to the stage measuring each step carefully. The applause faded as many gave up clapping long before she got to the stage.

Damian helped her across the stage and directed her in front of the Val-8. "What is your name, my dear?"

"Dorothy."

"Are you married, Dorothy?"

She shook her head. "My sweet Dennis passed away five years ago."

"Okay, I'm sorry to hear about your dentist," Stockwell said.

"Dennis," Dorothy said with a scowl that could only come from decades of marriage.

"I see. The Bertrand has been designed so you can boss him around just like any husband that isn't dead. Just tell it to do something. Go ahead and give it a try." He set the microphone in front of her.

"I don't know what to ask him," Dorothy said.

"What would you tell Dennis if he was here right now?"

"I'd ask him to fix us a cup of tea. He liked tea."

The Bertrand whirred and turned away from the crowd. The machine stepped into the model kitchen and scanned the room.

Wonderment spread through the crowd as the machine moved about, filling the kettle, setting it on the stove, pulling a teacup and saucer from the cabinet and preparing an infuser full of fresh tea leaves.

The kettle whistled and The Bertrand poured the water and steeped the tea. He set the cup on the saucer and returned to Dorothy.

She hesitated to take the cup but finally reached out and grabbed the teacup and saucer. She blew the steam aside and sipped at the cup. "It's delightful."

Damian spoke proudly into the microphone. "This is how we make tea in the future."

Fireworks launched from the foot of the stage and burst in the sky above them. The crowd applauded more than they had ever applauded tea.

The Val-8 held out an open hand. Inside its glove sat two sugar cubes, their crystalline structure glittering in the lights of the fair. "One lump or two, Madame?" it asked.

Dorothy shook her head. "None for me, thank you. I can't have sugar." She sipped the tea and smiled. "This is delici …"

The Val-8 closed its hand into a fist. Fine grains of sugar fell from its palm to the stage like the sands of time through an hourglass with a hole in the bottom. The Bertrand's eyes turned from soft blue to devil red. It reached out and closed its hand around Dorothy's neck eliciting a tiny squeak and gurgle as it pulled her from the chair and held her above the ground.

Dorothy kicked faster than she walked as she dangled at the machine's mercy.

Von Kempelen rushed to a nearby console and screamed for security as he manipulated a series of switches.

Uniformed men in dark gray rushed from the side of the stage and grabbed for the machine. One grabbed Dorothy around the waist and supported her weight while another grabbed the Val-8's arm and tried to pull her free. The third guard crossed a baton across The Bertrand's throat demonstrating little knowledge of how robots actually worked.

A single move from The Bertrand sent the security contingent flailing across the stage. Only the man under Dorothy was able to hold on.

Stockwell could see the blue-haired old woman turning into a blue-faced old woman before his eyes. He had to act before Dorothy joined her dentist husband in the great beyond. He tore the microphone from its stand and let the heavy device drop to the ground while pulling the length of cable through his hands.

He began to sway the weighted end inches from the floor and it quickly built up speed. He turned the pendulum's rhythm into a full swing and the mic spun around him. The roar of movement pumped through the PA system and filled the showcase with a demon's roar.

The crowd had quickly moved from awe to panic and their gasps of astonishment were now gasps of terror as they feared for Dorothy's life. The roar of the microphone silenced them as they became entranced by Stockwell's movements.

Damian moved fluidly, spinning and stepping in and out of the trailing cord as if dancing with the device. The cable wrapped around him at several angles, laced about every limb, all but binding him in place. The microphone had run out of cable and fell to rest in his hand.

Damian spoke into the microphone and his voice boomed over the crowd. "Hey, The Bertrand."

The Val-8 looked at the man who had tangled himself in microphone cable.

"Let her go," Damian said. With one last flourish, Stockwell spun sideways through the air and extended his right arm towards the Val-8. The microphone exploded from his hand like a bullet and howled through the air before striking the Val-8's face with a plastic crack and bouncing into Dorothy's face with an old lady grunt.

The Bertrand released the woman and turned towards Stockwell as its face and Dorothy fell to the floor. The Bakelite mask clattered on the stage.

Bertrand rushed in and slid beneath Dorothy as she fell to the ground. The Frenchman broke her fall and pulled her clear of the robot's footsteps.

The Bertrand faceplate was designed to appear nonthreatening, comforting even. The design team felt it was necessary as the Val-8's true face would frighten children and adults alike. The glowing red eyes were set among a thousand gears, springs and wires that were placed for efficiency, not aesthetics.

Stockwell looked into the monster's guts. Gears spun and whirred. The wires ran like veins throughout the head creating depth and shadows found only in nightmares. The machine set its glowing coals of hate on Stockwell as the man snapped the cord bringing the microphone back into his hand.

The security guards came at the machine again. They struck with batons and aching fists in every effort to stop the threat posed to the crowd, but these blows did nothing to slow the machine's stride.

Pistons fired and relays snapped as the Val-8 struck back at them with broad swipes that sent each man sprawling into the crowd or farther into the model home.

"Shut it down, von Kempelen!" Stockwell held the microphone tightly in his hand, knowing the improvised weapon was all but useless against his foe.

The doctor mashed buttons, yanked levers and spun dials furiously to no avail. "It's not responding to my controls."

The Val-8 struck with the force of industrial equipment and sent Stockwell sliding across the stage and clattering into a mass of steel folding chairs in the abandoned orchestra pit. It quickly turned its attention to what was left of the crowd.

The audience had emptied but for a few people who were too shocked, too stunned or too stupid to move. They sat fixated by the horror that was playing out on the stage in front of them like it was a radio drama come to life, convinced, perhaps, that the theater's mythical fourth wall would protect them.

Damian landed amid a pocket of spectators. The machine stared at him and raised its hands like Shelley's monster.

The microphone was still in his hand and Stockwell gripped

the device in an ever-tightening fist while responding to the robotologist. "Then whose controls is it responding too?"

The doctor had to yell back. "Something is overriding the system. I'm not sure how."

Stockwell rolled his eyes as the Val-8 reached the edge of the stage. He looked at the microphone. He smiled and replied to the doctor, "That's something we're going to have to fix in the future."

On the verbal cue, the fireworks erupted along the front of the stage. A large fountain of sparks burst beneath The Bertrand's feet and engulfed the machine in flames. The fine wear of the butler combusted and fed the fire. Soon the machine stood in a pillar of fire.

Even through the blaze, Stockwell could see the red of the machine's demonic eyes staring at him. Studying him. They pierced the smoke and burned into him before suddenly moving up and beyond him.

The Val-8 leapt into the air. A trail of smoke streaked behind it as the movement fueled the fire with a rush of air.

Stockwell pulled an arm across his face and waited for the impact. But the machine was no longer after him. The trajectory had carried the robot well beyond him into the pavilion.

Damian untangled himself from the chairs and spun as he leapt to his feet. The machine and its trail of smoke turned north and ran into the fairgrounds.

Stockwell ran after it, shouting into the microphone for Bertrand to follow. He dropped the mic as it reached the end of its cord and turned north in pursuit of the menace.

4

Midway of Mayhem

Dropped in a desert with nothing but wits and will, Damian Stockwell could track a rattlesnake across a mountain of rock. A year spent living with the Crow tribe had provided him an education that no university could bestow. He had learned their ways, their language and their customs. And they had imparted upon him their wisdom, their ability to read the land and the name Giant White Pain, as the chief was prone to migraines and jokingly accused Damian's radiant blonde hair of being their cause. He assumed.

The ability to track man and beast across any terrain was perhaps the most important skill he had learned from the Crow. It had proved invaluable in his life as a grand adventurer. Many a villain had tried to shake the Titan of Truth, but their own movements betrayed them. An overturned pebble or a single thread of fabric on a branch could be their undoing. Some of his prey accused him of being able to hunt by smell. These skills were necessary in his line of work and had led to a case's resolution countless times. Now, however, he needed none of these skills, as tracking a blazing six-foot robot through a crowd of thousands didn't prove too difficult.

The acrid smell of burning plastics filled the air and stung at his nose. The fumes made his head swim as he followed precisely the Val-8's path of destruction and the screams rising through the Home and Industrial Group Pavilion.

He saw fear in every face and the look crushed something deep inside him. His intention had been to bring these now horrified people a future of leisure, free from stress and worry. The Val-8 was the first step to an enlightened world. Damian had hoped The Bertrand model would free the people of America from the toil of tedious housework and eliminate the countless chores.

There was little doubt in his mind that if the people were provided hours a day of free time they would use it to better themselves, their families and the world around them. Free to read. Free to study. Free to visit cultural centers. They would grow as citizens of planet Earth and contribute to humanity's rich culture through poetry, art, music, possibly pottery and more.

What should have been lovely singing voices were now terrified screams that tore at his conscience. The Bertrand was developed to make their world a brighter place—it was supposed to be an instrument of good released into the world as a benefit to mankind. Instead he had set it on fire and pointed it into a crowd.

Stockwell rushed through the pavilion following the trail of damage and panic, smiling only when he saw that the machine had made its escape through the Dahlia Society's central garden. Petals smoldered and Mrs. Davenshire fumed as the once colorful exhibit turned to ash. The older woman shot hatred at Damian through bloodshot eyes as he trampled the one surviving bloom in the course of his pursuit. A sweet aroma hung in the air.

In the distance, there was a new host of screams, and Stockwell ran on as Mrs. Davenshire began to screech and rant.

Bertrand, the actual Bertrand, took the brunt of her ire and Damian smiled as he heard the valet apologize. Always the gentleman, Bertrand's calm, doormat-like behavior had diffused more than one tense situation in the past. Ladies loved the French.

The giant man moved with such speed that the homes in the pavilion became a blur. Despite this, the captain-of-industry was always at work. His incredible mind took in the competition and their offerings as he weaved through the model neighborhood following the trail of thinning smoke. Plastic was everywhere: siding, flooring, wallpaper and artificial lawns were just a few of the offerings. DamIndustries was well ahead of the competition. He was convinced home automatonamation was the future, provided he could stop this one from killing anyone.

The screaming spread. Fairgoers scattered through the grounds as they ran from the Val-8. As the area of panic grew and the smoke faded, it became more difficult to pinpoint the robot's path.

Stockwell abhorred screaming. Screaming wasn't the sound of terror. Screaming was the call of the confused and the unprepared. Those that were prepared were never startled, and when faced with shock they reacted appropriately. Not with a shriek. Screaming was the body's way of telling the world, "This idiot right here didn't consider this. Ever." And it was evident now that not a single person in the crowd had prepared themselves for the sudden rampage of a six-foot flaming man-servant.

This widespread lack of preparedness now caused him concern. The Bakelite had burned off. The smoke was fading. And now the fleeing crowd had caused so much damage that tracking the machine would become difficult.

Stockwell slowed and listened, trying to hear through the chaos. Most of the crowd didn't know why they were screaming, and there was a difference in a knowledgeable scream and a scream born of contagion.

Bertrand caught up and the pair shared a brief look as they listened for a clue. Through the din and dismay, a fresh batch of screams broke. Tiny and distant, they pierced through the noise.

"Mon Dieu," Bertrand swore. "Eez zit children?"

Stockwell did not fault the Frenchman for his ignorance. He merely shook his head and said, "No. My God, no." He ran faster than before and called to Bertrand over his shoulder. "To the Midget Village!"

It may have been mankind's largest small-scale endeavor. The Midget Village was a fully functioning town, though it was built to a lesser scale. The community resembled an alpine village and the tiny streets were lined with tiny stores. Western Union ran a cable dispatch service from the village and employed miniscule messengers that flit about the fair in full uniform.

Stockwell had spent a fair amount of time roaming the streets of the village. He had smiled as half-sized hula dancers swayed to a third-scale uke. He had his hair trimmed by bantam barbers in the town's barber shop. He had even stood witness to a couple of miniature marriage ceremonies and applauded with delight as the new bride and groom began their lives together in the town square.

The Midget Village even had midget city hall where a midget mayor had the grand honor of serving the midget residents of the city. There were sixty of these residents in all, making the fair the largest little people population ever gathered in one place. In short, it was a big deal.

Now Stockwell feared for the citizens of the tiny town as the robot would seem at least twenty-five to thirty percent more menacing to them. He moved against the tide of terror as fairgoers fled the midway and began to run faster when the oncoming crowd turned to a flow of Lilliputians. But even he would have to admit that he may have fallen prey to a trick of the eye and that, perhaps, it only seemed like he was running faster. Whichever the case, he trod more carefully and cautioned his valet. "Watch your shins, Bertrand!"

The three-quarter scale grand entrance to the village was a cobblestone arch made entirely of wood and paint that forced most visitors to the fair to bow their heads before entering the village. Despite its pedigree and gentlemanly programming, the Val-8 had obviously refused to bow and the archway was now only a fallen façade of splintered wood.

Damian stepped through the debris and was momentarily lost in a sense of perspective. Due in part to his great physical stature, he often looked down on people, but he was never prepared for the disproportionate feeling that overcame him once inside the half-sized hamlet.

Towering over the doorways—and in some cases the buildings themselves—he moved through the streets, careful not to touch the structures as he feared they might fall. As he cautiously rounded a corner into the town's square, a policeman struck him in the chest.

His reflexes would make a jungle cat jealous. They took over and Damian snagged the officer from the air, stopping his flight. He lowered the Midget City constable to his feet and noted that the man only rose to the bottom of his ribcage.

The patrolman looked up at the giant of good and pointed back to the square from which he had just been tossed. "Well, get in there, you big freak."

Damian smirked and dashed around the corner to see the entire force of diminutive deputies doing their best to topple the, relative to them, giant robot. Tiny cops were flying everywhere.

Those that weren't airborne beat against the robot's now exposed skeleton with three-quarter billy clubs. The clanging of varnished wood on metal did little but splinter the clubs and frustrate the cops. But despite their rising tempers, the men in uniform fought on.

Stockwell had witnessed courage in many forms, but he had never seen a display of this relative magnitude. The American spirit was alive and well in this tiny town.

An officer soared through the air and broke through the upper facade of the barbershop as the Val-8 grabbed yet another by the collar and lifted him from the ground.

Stockwell boomed, "Unhand that officer, you fiend!" His voice was the envy of baritones the world over. His control was impeccable and his projection unmatched. But it had never seemed so loud or large as it did in the town square of the Midget Village.

The shout was followed by silence as the melee stopped. The officers and the android turned towards Damian. The officers wore a look of surprise. The android wore the look of a half-melted French valet, as what was left of Bertrand's image dripped down its face.

"Drop the cop, The Bertrand," Stockwell commanded.

The Bertrand's voice projector had been damaged in the fire and no longer spoke in a refined French accent. The machine roared a burst of static. It crackled and spat what was most likely intended to be a string of French curses.

Bertrand arrived behind Stockwell as the unintelligible vulgarities ended and the Val-8 launched the cop into the air.

Damian dove forward and tucked into a roll that took him out of the airborne officer's path. He leapt back to his feet as the policeman struck Bertrand in the chest.

The Frenchman yelped as he and the officer crashed through the plate glass window of the Midget City Market. A bakery display of fresh baked loaves of bread cushioned the valet's fall while the valet cushioned the police officer's fall, preventing any serious impact injuries. The shards of glass still hurt.

Stockwell did not allow himself to become distracted by the shattering glass. His steel gray eyes were locked on his opponent as it roared static and feedback once more.

Their batons still in hand, the Midget Town Police Force stopped and looked to Damian for orders.

"You've done your duty, Officers. Leave this mechanical menace to me."

The cops looked at one another and backed away from the machine with caution until they were standing behind Stockwell. Two of the men turned and helped Bertrand and the other officer out of the window.

The sergeant was bruised. His uniform was torn, and he held only half a baton in his fist, but his courage had suffered no trauma. "You sure you've got this?"

Stockwell nodded. "Yes, Sergeant. You and your men have done all you can. Go now and know that you've protected your tiny town with the courage and honor of men twice your size."

"Did you hear that, Larry?" the sergeant asked one of the other men in blue.

"I sure did, Sarge." Larry slid his baton into the ring on his equipment belt.

"What do you think?"

"I didn't know they made assholes that big, Sarge."

"That's what I was thinking. Get Danny out of the bread racks and let's get out of here. We'll let Goliath take care of it."

Bertrand stepped out of the shattered window and moved beside Stockwell as the Midget City Police Force filed out of the town square, mumbling insults at the two men.

"What did you zay to zem, Monsieur?"

"I thought I complimented them."

"Zey do not zeem complimented."

Damian shook his head. "It doesn't matter, Bertrand. Those are fine men, and I'll have words with anyone who says different. For their badges may be small, but their hearts are big."

"Ah, you probably zaid somezing like zat."

The Bertrand crackled and popped and the two men turned to face the monster they had unleashed upon the fair. The glass eyes that had given it a human appearance were gone, and now it stared at them through the black eye of a mechanical lens.

Damian stared back. "What are you going to do now, The Bertrand? The officers are gone. You have nothing left to throw."

"Please do not taunt ze machine. I don't want you to make it angry."

Damian turned and crossed his arms across his chest. "Don't be silly, Bertrand. The Val-8 may appear intelligent, but it is nothing more than a collection of programs. It can't think. It can't feel. It doesn't have emotions. All it can do is respond to commands."

"Did you command it to tear up ze statue?"

"Of course not." Damian turned to see the Val-8 tearing up the town's water fountain.

The machine ripped the statuary featuring frolicking midgets from the fountain top and hurled it towards the two men. The pair fell to the ground as the stonework flew over their heads and crashed through what was left of the Midget Village Market.

Stockwell was on his feet in an instant and rushed across the square. The village had suffered enough. It was time to put a stop to the robot's rampage. The Val-8 swung at him and Damian ducked under the blow. He came up and met the machine's melted face with a right cross that succeeded only in removing the rest of the Bakelite mask. He struck again with a left and threw two shots to the body before the machine struck back.

This single blow sent the adventurer stumbling back across the square into Bertrand, who had just gotten to his feet. As the pair fell back to the ground, the machine crashed through a building and disappeared from the town square.

The two men stood. Stockwell made a fist and grimaced.

"What eez wrong, Monsieur?"

"I … I can't punch it. It's too hard. It's like punching …"

"Solid metal?" Bertrand asked.

"Yes, it's just like punching me."

"What can we do?"

Stockwell looked at his hands. He took a deep breath and shrugged.

A fresh chorus of screams erupted somewhere beyond the midway. Stockwell winced as he balled his fists tighter. "Bertrand, go get the car."

5

Fan Dance of Death

The world may indeed be a stage, but as the streets of the Midget Village twisted and turned into narrow pathways that ran among the castle walls of the Belgium exhibit, Stockwell mused that Chicago had become the stage for that world's stage. He smiled at his own cleverness and nearly tripped on a raised cobblestone.

He recovered from the near stumble and dashed through the medieval corridors toward the sound of the screams before bursting into the pavilion's courtyard. He expected a crowd of panicked fairgoers to be running over one another seeking freedom from harm, but this crowd knew how to panic.

There was indeed a crowd. The pavilion was at capacity, but the men and women didn't scramble, scream or even stir. They sat patiently in their seats allowing the chaos to rage on about them as it wished. They were having no part of it.

His entrance drew the attention of the hundreds seated

inside. They looked up from their beers, and Stockwell's confusion dissipated. Before each visitor sat a glass of beer—some of the first legal brew available to the nation since the repeal of Prohibition a few days prior. A simple rampaging robot was not nearly enough to make them leave their seats.

The crowd wasn't so far from sobriety, however, that they couldn't put two and two together. They pointed en masse towards the entrance to the Spanish Village.

A few broken steins and weeping men confirmed that it was the path The Bertrand had taken. Stockwell grabbed a nearby stein, lifted it to the crowd and downed the ale in a single swig. Freedom tasted sweet. He acknowledged the applause with another raise of the glass and ran on as the stein's owner grumbled.

The Spanish Village was in a more expected level of disarray as the nation was not serving beer. The appropriately panic-stricken crowd screamed, ran about and yelled about nothing helpful at all. Some tried scrambling up the adobe walls in their attempts to flee. They vaulted over the rounded walls and sought refuge behind the clay brick.

Damian arrived in the villa's courtyard as the Val-8 demonstrated that clay brick, while an energy efficient and suitable building material for an arid environment, wasn't the best choice for impeding the rampage of a robot.

Red dust filled the pavilion as the machine made short work of the walls and gravity took care of the rest. The panicked screams turned to gasps and coughs as the dust made its way into the crowd.

Stockwell filled his cavernous lungs with a final breath of clean air and walked into the thickening cloud. The more the Val-8 destroyed, the harder it was to see.

There was a crunch to his left and a crash louder than the others. The noise carried on as part of a structure collapsed. He ran toward the sound as the cloud of dust thinned and whisked away on the opposite side of a hole in the village wall. Damian stepped through the rubble and found himself outside of the Italian Village which, naturally, looked like an airplane.

Unlike the other countries, the Italians had chosen to construct their village to showcase less of their heritage and more of their future. An aviation demonstration scheduled for later in the year was intended to show off their aeronautical prowess, and the nation had chosen to have their architecture reflect the growing industry.

One look at the structure, however, and Damian, looking through the eye of an accomplished engineer, was convinced it wouldn't fly.

Rather than destroying another pavilion, The Bertrand raced down the pathway that ran along the north pond as the crowd parted before it.

Concerned only with how it moved about the home, the lab had never clocked the machine's speed on open ground. But it was apparent now that it was considerable. Stockwell's feet pounded the asphalt with a practiced frenzy that he had employed a thousand times before to catch fleet-footed felons, but it was not enough, and he quickly fell behind the machine.

Undeterred, he did not slow. He passed the boat show and the building advertising Live Babies in Incubators where the miracle of life met the miracle of plastics as premature infants were tended to in front of a paying audience.

The Bertrand was forced to slow when it reached the crowd at the Pabst Blue Ribbon building. Much like the visitors at the Belgium castle, the people here were not giving up their ground so easily. Even with the Hall of Religion across the way looming over them, those in line shouted at the machine to get to the back or get something else much less pleasant.

Stockwell received the same treatment when he arrived a moment later. Now, upset by the gall of the robot to cut in line, the crowd was less than willing to step aside and let him through. They formed a wall of flesh and slurs and it was only Damian's great height that permitted him to see The Bertrand continue down the pathway to the base of the Sky Ride.

Built to rival the iconic status of the Eiffel Tower, a committee toiled for months to develop something that would trump the Paris World's Fair landmark. In the end there was only one answer to the question, "What's better than a giant steel tower?" That answer was, of course, two giant steel towers. And rocket cars. Two thousand tons of American steel made up the twin towers of the attraction. Each tower measured more than six hundred feet, and there were more than eighteen hundred feet between them. This distance was crossed by fairgoers and adventure seekers in one of twelve double-decker rocket cars that had been pulled from the pages of the future. Each one left behind it a trail of rocket smoke as they traversed the fair's lagoon.

The twin sentinels rose above the tallest buildings in Chicago and stood as a testament to America's ingenuity, ability and dedication to never finishing in second place. They were beacons for an entire generation embroiled in a depression. A symbol that said if you throw enough money at a problem, you can easily pretend that problem is no longer there. It was something the entire country could be proud of. And now it was being scaled by a potentially murderous robot that Stockwell had helped create.

Time for courtesy had run out. Damian burst through the thirsty crowd, leaving them to hurl insults and a few stones at his back as he rushed to the base of the tower.

The Val-8 ascended quickly. Its metal bones clashed with the steel girders, creating sparks against the Sky Ride structure as it went. But this spectacle was nothing compared to the ride itself.

As the sun set, each rocket car was lit from the ground. These massive spotlights gave the ride an otherworldly feel and, combined with the illuminated steam that poured from each vehicle, captured the complete attention of those on the ground. The crowd outside the elevator stood with their necks craned skyward and their eyes directed to the cars suspended over the lagoon. Lost in a fog of fantasy and wonderment, they hadn't even noticed the Val-8.

Damian ran into the crowd and began to shout. "I need to get to the elevator. Let me through."

The crowd took their attention from the sky and began to shout back.

"Like hell, buddy. I've been waiting for two hours."

"Wait your own turn."

"Get in line."

"You don't understand," he countered. "There's a potentially dangerous robot on the loose."

With this, they laughed.

"Looks like this guy's been spending too much time at Pabst."

"Maybe he's been reading a little too much science fiction."

"Maybe he's just a big stupid idiot who's dumb and not too much smart." This came from a child and it hurt the most.

Their insults were lost as the crowd worked itself from a tither into a frenzy. Damian ignored them and looked back at the tower. He could no longer see the machine. The Bertrand had disappeared somewhere in the structure.

Stockwell backed away from the tower and the burgeoning mob to see higher into the air. He saw it. The Val-8 had already made the lower platform. Damian cursed as he watched the machine move hand over hand across the cable towards one of the rocket cars suspended over the lagoon. Even the elevator wasn't fast enough to catch The Bertrand now.

He turned and dashed back along the shoreline and red-rovered his way through the beer line, spilling the thirsty, shouting patrons across the asphalt walkway. As he ran, he kept The Bertrand in his peripheral vision and his destination straight ahead.

The Century of Progress Boat Show featured myriad crafts. Rubber boats made by Chrysler ferried passengers across the lagoons. Yachts much smaller than his were on display for the green eyes of the middle-class and those from landlocked states. Damian ran down the dock past all of these crafts to a grouping of much smaller boats. Shaped like a manta ray and no bigger than a man, they were designed for one reason—to win the National

Outboard Association's High Point trophy. Equipped with powerful outboard motors and designed to slice through the lake at more than eighty miles an hour, they were the joy and potential pride of the men that raced them. Damian was surprised they weren't being watched more closely.

He untied the closest craft and, with a mighty shove from the dock, sent the boat drifting into the harbor. He leapt into the cockpit with such authority that even the owner would not question that he belonged at its controls. One pull of the cord and the outboard barked to life. Stockwell grabbed the throttle and opened it wide.

The man-made lagoons may have calmed the motion of the lake, but the small craft still found every wave and valley in the water until the propeller caught up to Stockwell's haste. Piloting such a craft took a practiced skill and complete concentration. Damian watched the Sky Ride as he flew across the lagoon.

The Bertrand was now moving atop the rocket car. If its goal was to cause destruction, it could easily release the passenger gondola and, driven by gravity and theatrical rocket steam, let it plummet to the water below.

The machine stomped across the roof of the second deck. The noise must have terrified the passengers inside. But, to Stockwell's relief, the robot did not tamper with the fasteners. It moved across the roof, grabbed the cable and continued on its way.

Damian wondered again about the Val-8's newfound purpose. He didn't like unanswered questions. They festered in the back of his magnificent mind and never let him alone until they were answered. Why had the Val-8 turned evil? Were these actions its own doing? Was sabotage to blame? Had some foreign agent or industrial competitor fouled its benevolent purpose with a corrupt code of ethics? Was someone else in control? It had to be someone else's doing. To his knowledge there was no rampage protocol within the Val-8's programming.

His quest for an answer led him to consider allowing The Bertrand to go its way. Following it would tell him, at the very least, where it was trying to go. Even this would give him a clue to its motive.

The Bertrand beat him across the water and moved onto the second steel structure. Many feet above the Sky Ride was an observation platform filled with spectators just waiting to be threatened and terrified. Panic at great heights was always dangerous. People tended to shove and fall, and that almost always made the papers.

The boat skipped off a wave at seventy miles an hour and the boat flew from the surface of the lagoon as Stockwell relaxed. The Val-8 was making its way to the ground. The boat landed with a thwack Stockwell felt in his knees, but he powered on towards the opposite shore.

The Bertrand would be on the ground soon. It wasn't climbing down but dropping from crossbeam to crossbeam.

Damian veered left towards the foot of a massive tower and pointed the speeding boat straight towards an inflatable Chrysler that had just motored from the dock. The automotive company had several ferries in the lagoon to transport passengers while doing its best to enter the marine market.

These passengers screamed as the ferry captain cut hard to port, sending his fares collapsing to their right. The abrupt turn in the high-walled laden craft threw up a tremendous wake.

The Val-8 dropped to the ground and moved north along the shore.

Stockwell struck the Chrysler's wake and launched the runabout from the water.

Not surprising to him, his timing was perfect. Damian leapt from the boat as it collided with the robot. He rolled into the soft bank of the lagoon as the machines twisted together and scraped across the asphalt pathway running next to the lake.

Sparks sprung to life as the propeller scraped the hard surface. Within seconds, the fuel in the boat's engine burst into flames.

Stockwell turned his back to the eruption and began to move

the gathering crowd to safety. "Back up, everyone. There's nothing to see here."

The crowd, as crowds are apt to do, didn't listen.

"Move along, please. Everything amazing that was going to happen has happened. Please enjoy the fair. I invite you to visit the DamIndustries Pavilion. It's the home of tomorrow, you know."

Someone in the crowd screamed, and Stockwell turned back to the burning wreckage.

The Val-8, burned to its metal skeleton, hoisted the flaming watercraft above its head.

"Are you kidding me?" Stockwell screamed. "I hit you with a damn boat!"

Motors spun and pistons pumped as The Bertrand heaved the burning hulk into the crowd.

Stockwell had trained hard to move faster than pneumatics. He sprang into the crowd first and tackled a young woman who stood in the path of the missile. The boat crashed behind them as the crowd finally scattered.

He looked at the woman in his arms and recognized the look she gave him. She was terrified, relieved, enamored and considering a lawsuit all at once. She wanted to scream but was lost in his eyes. His eyes had cost him precious moments in situations like this before. He'd curse them, if they weren't his mother's.

She couldn't speak—whether it was love or the wind had been struck from her lungs, he couldn't be sure—but she mouthed the words, "Thank you."

A new crowd began to scream as the machine moved south through the fairgrounds.

Damian stood quickly and surveyed the area. The machine was gone. How long had the woman been lost in his eyes?

There was a mob running from the Hollywood pavilion and he ran against its flow. He excused himself as he shoved people out of the way and pardoned himself for any bruises he may have left as they collided with him. The Val-8 had to be inside. Crowds had shoved and pushed to get into the Hollywood pavilion since its opening, but never to leave. It contained the single biggest attraction the fair, and thus the world, had to offer.

And there she was. She didn't flee the building. She danced her way from the doors down the steps, wearing nothing but feathers. She swayed and sauntered right into his arms.

He smiled.

She slapped him.

"What was that for, Sally?"

"For all the things you've been saying about us in the papers," she said with a smile.

"I haven't been saying anything."

"Exactly. I have a reputation to uphold."

"I'd say your reputation is holding up just fine. You've caused quite a stir here."

"There's no such thing as too much press. You know that."

"Then I think I can help us both." Stockwell leaned in towards her as Sally Rand closed her eyes and pursed her lips.

Damian grabbed the world-famous feathered fans from the dancer's hand and rushed towards the building. "I'll bring these back."

She yelled something at him as he ran. It was probably something about him leaving her standing there fanless and naked. He guessed it could have been something else, but that was his best guess at the moment.

Sally Rand's infamous fan dance was both the biggest attraction and the biggest source of controversy at the fair. She drew crowds of spectators and heaps of criticism for her scandalous yet captivating performance. Even in the early days of the fair it was clear that the spectators were less interested in the countless cultural displays from around the globe than they were in seeing Sally's globes displayed.

The inside of the Hollywood pavilion was a wreck. Trash from the concession stands littered the ground, and his feet mashed popcorn into the ornate carpet as he made his way across the silent lobby. The mess was the only sign of the Val-8, but he could tell that the machine wasn't far. Damian could sense when he was being watched, and it intrigued him to discover that this ability extended to mechanical devices.

"I know you're in here, The Bertrand." Was there any reasoning with a machine? "I don't know why you're doing this, but I've got to say you've piqued my curiosity."

There was a crash from the top of the grand staircase. Stockwell turned in that direction but still couldn't see the machine.

"Why don't you come with me and we'll fix whatever is wrong with you?"

The Bertrand was not designed to scream, but the static and crackle of its voice amplification module roared, popped and hissed as the machine leapt from the staircase and crashed to the ground in front of its creator.

The entirety of its human appearance had been burned away by the fire on the shore. The synthetic hair was gone, revealing a soot-covered and tarnished metal skull. The plastic that had covered its face and neck remained only as charred clumps of black tar. Bertrand's suit was an apology he'd have to make later.

"You've caused enough destruction." Stockwell pointed at the machine with his intimidation finger. The effect was only slightly lessened by the giant four-foot feathers he held in his hand. "Are you ready to come in?"

The Val-8's eyes whirred back and forth as the feathers bounced. Its head began to sway. The machine roared.

Stockwell smiled. "Fine. Let's dance."

The Bertrand lunged as Damian spun and brought the burlesque fans in front of his face. Ages ago, the samurai had used fans in war. Stockwell had studied the art and employed its teachings now. The samurai fans were made of metal, and the feathers swayed more than he would have thought. But each time a feather fluttered, the Val-8's eyes struggled to find their focus.

The Bertrand charged again and the dance began in earnest.

Stockwell spun and ducked. He leapt and leaned. Keeping the feathers in constant motion kept The Bertrand off balance. The more he moved, the more the machine stumbled.

He moved toward the door. Stockwell chuckled as one of the feathers brushed his chin.

The Val-8 rushed as Damian stepped aside, and the robot crashed through the door back into the fairgrounds. Damian, armed with the feathers, followed.

Crowds don't run for long. They only flee until they are certain they are not being pursued, then they turn into spectators. Stockwell emerged to a roar of laughter. In his hands, the infamous feathers had to look ridiculous. He felt himself begin to blush a little as pride rushed to the surface of his skin. He fought it back. Though his image may suffer, it was for the greater good.

The dance continued. Damian twirled to the delight of the crowd and the confusion of the machine. It was becoming predictable now. He was finally back in control of his company's creation. He spun and drove it left into a column, then pirouetted and watched it crash through the barker's booth.

The crowd's laughter turned to cheers as he choreographed The Bertrand to the shore of the lagoon. There it stopped.

"Into the water, you foul contraption." He lunged at the robot with both fans but it refused to move. Somehow it knew that the water would be its demise.

Stockwell pushed forward again and the machine lunged through the fans and, grabbing the man by the wrists, it pulled itself through the feathers until it was eye to eye with the feather dancer. The eyes whirred and finally found their focus. The Val-8 pulled the fans away and grabbed Damian by the neck.

Static rumbled from the robot's chest as it lifted the adventurer from the ground and held him over the water.

"So the fans won't work, huh?" He felt the machine begin to squeeze. "Guess I'll have to hit you with a car."

The roar of a V-16 was a totally unique sound and had never before been heard outside of GM's factory. Though distinct, it was enough to grab the Val-8's attention.

The long black car tore across the asphalt, its horn and lights blazing a path through the crowd.

Damian fell to the ground as The Bertrand turned its focus on the other Bertrand behind the wheel.

Stockwell dove out of the way as Bertrand drove into The Bertrand. The hood crumpled and the machine flew back into the lagoon.

The Val-8 thrashed about as the water seeped into its housing and short-circuited its electrical system. One final burst of garbled static came through a waterlogged speaker and the machine stopped. It stood waist deep in the water, silent and still.

Bertrand shut the car door and swore at the machine.

Damian stood, brushed the fight from his palms and strode towards the car. "Nice work, my good friend. You did exactly as I …" Damian stopped and looked at the Cadillac limousine. "This is not my car."

"Non, Monsieur."

"This is the car from the auto show."

"Oui, Monsieur. It was clozer."

"It is a nice car, though."

"Drives like a dream," Bertrand said.

"Really? Do you think I should buy one?"

"I zink you just deed, Monsieur."

6

Drink of Despair

The Chicago chapter of the Vagabond Club reeked of new. Less than a year old, the honored society had been forced to furnish the newly constructed space with pieces that were less than storied. Unlike the New York chapter, there was no history to the chair in which Damian sat. It didn't come from an emperor's throne room. It was not unearthed from a sacred tomb. It was never carted across the Dark Continent on a safari by a noted big game hunter. It was simply a chair. And that was unfortunate.

His personal fortune had paid for the club's construction, and as soon as he was home, he'd send part of his personal collection to help with the decor. Replica maps and imitation antiques were not befitting of the club's standing. Looking around the room, it pained him to see the money he had spent on such pageantry.

Of course, that amount was nothing compared to what DamIndustries would have to pay to repair the damage to the fair.

The thought of rebuilding Spain alone made him grip the glass of whiskey a little tighter. How could dried mud cost so much? It was just mud. He could more than afford the cost, but the circumstances depressed him more than any amount of money could.

It was his idea, his creation, that had turned the exposition of optimism into an experiment in terror. He was embarrassed by the machine's failure. The story had made the front page of the late edition. Many in the crowd, who earlier were too ill-prepared to do anything but scream, were more than happy to speak about their harrowing experience. And it did not surprise him in the least to read Ted Starr's name in the byline.

The drink in his hand was new as well. The fully stocked bar arrived within hours of the Volstead Act's repeal, thanks to good friends in the club's Canadian chapter. Hours after the bar was filled with booze, the club was filled with Vagabonds.

Though he didn't know their names or their personal histories, he knew every face. The Vagabond committee had to approve of every member as a rule of charter. As the club had expanded around the world, getting to know each candidate personally had become prohibitive, and they came to rely on the referrals of other members. It was not his preferred method. He liked to know everyone, but he had no one but himself to blame.

His exploits around the globe had not only brought attention to the storied fraternity, they inspired many to seek adventures of their own. The club had never had a shortage of applicants, but more were qualified than ever before.

The Vagabond Club was his second home, if you didn't count the numerous second homes he actually owned around the world. It was a familiar place in a foreign city that offered him and his fellow Vagabonds a friendly place to rest, resupply, gather local information and even stay if necessary. But with every strange face, it felt less and less like it was supposed to.

An elderly member sat across from him in the imitation antique Queen Anne chair and sipped at a whiskey with more caution than most in the room. While the others rushed through each drop, the old man slurped loudly and, mixing air with the amber liquid, held it in his mouth. His cheeks danced as he passed the sip from side to side, and Damian could see a look of delight with every note of taste he discovered. The man noticed Stockwell watching, raised his glass and offered an explanation.

"This is the first drink I've had in fifty years. And I'm going to savor every damn drop."

Damian smiled and raised his glass.

"Have you got the same plan? You've hardly touched your drink."

Stockwell looked at the drink in his hand. He was no teetotaler. The temperance movement was something he never fully understood. He had made a life out of helping others, saving people from peril when endangered by man or nature. But he rarely saw it as his job to save anyone from themselves, no matter how much he disapproved of what they were doing. He believed that as long as they weren't hurting anyone else, it was between them and God. The idea that a group of people would force their own will on another was everything he stood against, whether it was "for their own good" or not. He had looked forward to the repeal of the draconian law as much as any other red-blooded American. But, now that it was here, he simply did not feel like drinking.

"Did you lose your taste for it?" asked the older man.

Damian shook his head. "It's just been a long day."

"Well, I can fix that." The old man raised his glass again. "Here's to long days." He smiled and sipped. After a few moments of savoring, he added, "You sure look like you've lost something. What was it?"

Stockwell chuckled and dragged a hand down his face. "A butler."

"I'm sorry to hear that, son. There's a reason they say good help is hard to find. Because it is." He sipped some more and lost his focus for a moment. Satisfied with the experience of that particular sip, he swallowed it and continued. "That's the reason they say that. What was his name?"

"The Bertrand."

"Bertrand, eh? What happened? Did he quit?"

"Hardly. He wouldn't stop. I had to light him on fire, hit him with a Cadillac and throw him in a lake."

"I beg your pardon, son? It's not my place to tell a man how to treat his staff, but you are mighty hard on your help. There's other ways to discipline a man besides setting him on fire. Did you ever think of just docking his wages?"

"You don't understand. The Bertrand wasn't a person. He was a thing."

It was the first time the old man set his drink down. He pointed a long, thin finger and his voice dropped an octave. "People aren't possessions, son. They can't be kept. You'd best remember that."

"No, he was a literal thing. He wasn't alive. The Bertrand was an automaton. Designed and manufactured by the best robotologists in the world. But then he turned." Damian picked up the glass and took a swig of the blended whiskey. "He turned evil."

"So you killed him?"

"No, I didn't kill him."

"Son, if you set him on fire, hit him with a car and threw him into a lake, there's a good chance you killed him."

"I told you. He wasn't alive."

"And I'm asking you, who's to say what's living or not? What is alive, anyway? Life cannot be defined simply by the process of taking breaths. That's not what living is."

"It's a big part of it."

The old man laughed. It was a weak and tired laugh. "Hardly. I know many that breathe who are hardly living." He leaned forward in his chair, put a bony elbow on his knee and extended his right hand. "We haven't met, Mr. Stockwell, but I think you know who I am, since you were the one who invited me to join this fine club. My name is Ronald Cook, and I should start by saying thank you."

Damian did know the name, and he shook the offered hand. "It's an honor to finally meet you, Mr. Cook. And anyone who's searched for Trapalanda is more than qualified to be called a Vagabond."

The old man smiled and leaned back in his chair. He lifted the glass to his lips and stared into the drink. "I'm afraid I wasn't quite completely honest in my application."

"You didn't search for the lost city of Patagonia?"

"Not quite." He smirked. "I found it."

Stockwell spilled his whiskey as he shot forward to the edge of his seat. He tamed his excitement and whispered, "You found the City of the Caesars?"

Cook nodded and took a large sip. He didn't savor this one. It had purpose beyond taste.

Damian leaned in. "And you've told no one of this?"

The old man shook his head. "It's of no use. I can't go back. No one can go back."

"Surely we can mount an expedition."

"The city is gone forever. It destroyed itself upon my departure."

Stockwell sat back in the chair with a frown and took a shot of the whiskey. "I hate it when that happens."

"I tell you this story now only because I think you need to hear it. It was thirty years ago. I was a younger man then, though not as young as you are now. And I was foolish. Years earlier I had signed on with General Roca and his men and participated in the Conquest of the Desert. Their goal was to unite the country, but I went for the money. I didn't think much beyond myself at that time and figured a buck was a buck." He took another hard swallow. "But it didn't take long before I learned the difference. I quickly became disillusioned with the general's methods of unity, and deserted. But they followed."

The old man's eyes filled with the wonder of his own words as he continued. "It was during my flight from Roca's justice that I came across a valley high in the Andes. Where the Earth met the sky and where the glaciers met with mountains weeping lava. That constant struggle between fire and ice filled the valley with a mist so thick that a man could easily get separated from himself. This fog had concealed the city and its people from the world for ages."

"Its people?" Stockwell asked. "There were people?"

Ronald nodded again. "It's a bit misleading to say I discovered the city. Because in truth, they discovered me. In my haste to escape from my pursuers, I slipped on some ice and tumbled from a ledge. I fell forever into that canyon and felt every rock and root on the way to the bottom. I was hurt. I couldn't even stand. And I lost hope.

"I cried out and heard nothing but my own screams in reply. I lay there for hours." Cook took a drink. "It must have been my cries of agony that drew them to me. And if I hadn't been crying like a baby, I doubt they ever would have found me. It's not my proudest moment, but the people of The Wandering City found me in the fog and tended to my wounds."

Stockwell shook his head and smiled. "So did they take you in as a god or a prisoner? It's always one of the two. I prefer God myself. It seems a little blasphemous, I know, but I've always found it easier to convince them you're just a man than it is to get out of some of those dungeons."

"Neither. They took me in as a wounded traveler and nothing more. A fellow man. I was not the first they had rescued. Or the first they took in. Many men and women had come over the years. And they were almost always welcome."

Stockwell chuckled. "How long did it take you to get the language down? It usually takes me a week or so, depending on its roots." He laughed harder. "Until then, it's all pantomime, speaking slowly and drawing things in the dirt. And let me tell you, that can go wrong. One time I drew the chief holding a spear at waist level and when he looked at it he did not see a spear, I can tell you that much. I barely got out of there alive, and as soon I got back I got myself some art lessons."

"It took no time at all. We spoke the same language."

"So the legends are true?" Stockwell asked. "They spoke Spanish?"

"Yes. Trapalanda was settled by a host of sailors shipwrecked in the straights. And even more Spaniards came after their defeat at Curalaba."

"And the Patagonian Giants? And the ghosts as well?"

Ronald waved his hand at Stockwell's growing excitement. "Don't believe everything you read, my boy." He smiled wryly. "There's no such thing as ghosts."

"But if they took you in so willingly and you didn't accidentally draw the chief playing with his own thing, why did you have to escape?" Stockwell thought for a moment and smiled. "Uh oh. Someone fell in love."

Cook nodded. "Quickly and entirely. Her name was Reega. She was everything to me and I to her."

"Chief's daughter?"

"No. She was my caregiver during my recovery. My Florence Nightingale." The next drink emptied the glass and he raised his hand for another.

"But Reega was not the reason for my imprisonment. General Roca had sent men after me. Somehow they found their way through the fog to the city. They saw only its riches, not its beauty. They snuck away and in the course of a year formed an army of filibusters. Then they returned and tried to take the city by force."

The waiter set a full glass down next to Ronald, and he took half of it in a single gulp. "The fighting was fierce. Countless died in the struggle. The Trapalandians' weapons were outdated. They fought modern rifles with muskets and rusted cutlasses. Their warriors were poorly prepared. It was only through sheer numbers and the desire to defend their home that they prevailed."

"You've got to love the home team," Stockwell said, but his words were not heard. Cook was lost in his memories.

"But they held me responsible. I had led these men to the city. I was responsible for the bloodshed. I should have been put to death. It would have been best for everyone." He took another long drink. "But, as I had played no hand in the attack, they felt it would be wrong to kill me. They were good people. Kind and decent people. But they were still really, really pissed, and so they subjected me to their cruelest punishment. There's no word for it outside of Trapalanda. It was an internal exile. I was locked in a cell away from the city and people I had grown to love. I was fed well, but I was to see no one for the rest of my life."

"That is pretty harsh."

"Banishment I can handle. Loneliness can be suffered. The true punishment was what they placed in the cell with me."

Stockwell found his voice was only a whisper as he asked, "What was it?"

"It was Reega."

"Well, that's wonderful, because that's the girl you fell in love with."

Cook shook his head. "They carved her out of stone. A statue, a perfect likeness, to remind me every day of the love I could never have."

"Not so wonderful."

"But, and here's the point of my story so pay close attention, I spent decades with that statue ... with my Reega. Over the years she became more than stone. We talked. We embraced. We ... there was a hole in the back. We did everything together. When there was no one else, there was her." He took a long drink. "Do you see what I'm saying, son?"

Stockwell leaned away from the old man as far as the back of the chair would allow. "Yes. You did it with a statue."

"No, that's not what I'm ..."

"You said there was a hole."

"Well, yes, but that's not my point. She was alive. She didn't talk. She didn't move. She didn't breathe. She was a statue, but that didn't matter, because she was alive. Just like your butler."

Stockwell stood up. "Hey, I didn't do my robot butler."

"I think you're focusing on the wrong part of my story. My

point is, she was as alive to me as you are."

Damian pointed at the old man. What was left of his drink sloshed onto the floor. "Don't you go getting ideas about me, Mr. Cook. I'm sorry you lost your statue lover in the collapse of a mythological city. It happens to the best of us. You need to move on and get a new life. But don't think you're going to make me a very weird part of it."

Damian slammed his glass on the table and stormed out of the lounge. Once out of the room, he stopped and put his face in his hands.

An attentive staff member took note and approached. "Is everything all right, Mr. Stockwell?"

"Everything's fine." He pulled his hands away and took a breath. "Everything is just fine. Come here."

The staff member stepped closer and Damian put an arm around his shoulder and turned him towards the lounge.

"You see that old man over there in the burgundy Queen Anne?"

"I do, sir."

"Keep an eye on him."

"I will, sir."

"And keep him away from the statues."

"Do what, sir?"

"You heard me."

"Okay, sir."

Damian slapped the young staff member on the shoulder and made his way through the club, down the elevator, then outside onto the streets of Chicago, where he could breathe again.

It was late, but there was no shortage of traffic on the streets. New York may be the city that never sleeps, but Damian was certain Chicago didn't get to sleep until well after one.

"Hey there, Dam." The professional edge in her voice was gone. Even her posture had changed from prim and proper to comfortable and casual. She leaned against a parked car as the Windy City tossed strands of hair across her face. They didn't seem to bother her and they were doing all the right things for him.

He smiled. "Ms. Palmer."

"Please, Dam. I've been traveling with you for how long now? Call me Angelica."

"Angelica." She smiled when he said her name. "What brings you out so late?"

"I couldn't sleep." She pushed herself from the car and walked slowly towards him. The sway of her step made her path less a direct line and more of a slow and gentle curve. "I guess it's all of the excitement from today. If every day is this exciting for you, I can't imagine you ever get much rest."

Damian shrugged. "You might be surprised to hear that chasing an unstoppable machine through a large crowd of men, women and children has left me a tad sleepy."

"Oh, really?" She stepped in front of him.

He nodded. The brim of his hat flicked against hers and turned it slightly askew. Her perfume was a delightful bouquet that he had never noticed on her before. Sweet and floral but with an edge in it he couldn't quite place.

She straightened her hat. "Then why don't we go back to your place and you can tell me all about it. Maybe we can end this news story with an exclamation point."

Damian whistled for a cab and a driver pulled over immediately. He opened the door and held it for Angelica. As she passed by him, he added, "I hope you're talking about sex."

She smiled like she was talking about sex.

7

Laboratory of Lies

The presidential suite at the Drake Hotel was designed to keep the most persistent assassin out. For this very reason, heads of state and royalty from around the world had stayed in the opulent residence since it opened a decade before. It could keep the world's most important people safe from harm, but it seemed it could not keep the sun out of their eyes.

The eastern morning sun draped across him and he awoke alert. Sleep was an ally that refreshed and healed, but sleepiness was an enemy of the vigilant, a nemesis of the prepared. Long ago he had made allies of one and done away with the other. Damian had trained his body and mind to reap the benefits of sleep while rejecting the detriments of the waking process. For him, there was no state in between the two. He simply went from fast asleep to fully aware.

There was no question of where he was. He never awoke in

such a stupor. He knew instantly his exact location, down to precisely which side of the room he was facing. He rolled over knowing that he faced east and stretched out his arm into an empty bed. The place where she had slept wasn't even warm. He opened his eyes to find himself alone in the room.

"She left?" Damian smiled and took in a satisfied breath. Her perfume still hung in the air. "Damn, that's sexy."

He didn't roll out of bed like most men. Stockwell rolled out of bed and dropped to the floor for a quick one hundred push-up warm-up. Once complete, he rolled into several different positions and completed a full hour's workout in less than three minutes. He made a quick call to have Bertrand bring the car around before stepping into a cold shower and getting dressed. He whistled as he buttoned his shirt.

The staff of the Drake fussed over him as he made his way from the suite and through the lobby. Was everything to his liking? How was he enjoying his trip? Wasn't it a beautiful day? His only response was to hold up the paper he had found outside his door and let them read the headline for themselves: DamIndustries Debacle! Mechanical Menace Fouls Fair.

It wasn't like him to sulk, but he felt directly responsible for the danger and destruction at the expo, and it was clear that the papers and the public agreed.

They called his creation the dream of a reckless industrialist. They said he was a capitalist without a cause, concerned only about the dollar and not for the safety of his consumers. They said his actions would cast the fair into financial ruin, and he alone should be responsible for the damages.

He couldn't disagree with them on that point. He had already found himself culpable, and had his team assess the damages. He tucked the paper under his arm with a grunt. It wasn't the money that bothered him. It was the failure. He had to find out what went wrong.

He found it rather warm out on the street despite the breeze off the lake. He could hear the bustle from Michigan Avenue. The

Drake's entrance had been situated on Walton Street to accommodate automobile traffic, and he was thankful the crowds were around the corner.

Bertrand was waiting outside the entrance with the Duesenberg and opened the car door as he approached. "Bonjour, Monsieur."

"What's so good about it?" Stockwell snapped as he tossed the paper into the rear seat. "Tell me one thing." He stepped into the limo and pulled the door shut himself.

Bertrand merely harrumphed, closed the door and took his seat behind the wheel.

Once the door was closed, Stockwell spoke, "I'm sorry I snapped at you, my friend."

"I've zeen ze papers, Monsieur. I underztand."

Damian picked up the paper just so he could throw it across the car again. "Why? Who? How? These questions have been eating at my mind all night, like some parasite that can't be sated."

"I trust not all night, Monsieur," Bertrand said with a wink in the rearview mirror.

Damian smiled and asked, "What do you mean?"

"I zaw Ms. Palmer leaving earlier zis morning."

Stockwell chuckled. His French friend was right. His mind had not been completely consumed by the mishap at the fair. "She made grammar sexy, Bertrand. No woman has ever done that for me."

This thought kept the smile on his face as they made their way through Chicago to the DamIndustries Robotology Laboratory in the city's industrial center.

Established solely as a staging ground for the Val-8 presentation, the warehouse bore no external markings and was purchased under a subsidiary company to keep the project a secret from the press and the competition. Even Angelica, who had been granted special access to Damian and the project, was not aware of its location or existence.

That secrecy was even more critical now. Damian instructed

Bertrand to park down the street from the facility. The pair would walk from there.

He stepped from the car and made a casual sweep of the street to ensure they had not been followed. This was done mostly out of habit. Bertrand was an excellent driver and could shake a tail with such proficiency that the tail would never even know they had been spotted in the first place. On a good day he could get them following someone else.

The valet joined Stockwell on the sidewalk, and they began the walk to the warehouse on the cracked and broken slabs.

"Do you have any idea what may have happened with ze robot?" Bertrand asked.

"I have several ideas," Stockwell said. "And I don't like any of them."

"What do you zink went wrong with ze machine?"

"Nothing. The machine acted perfectly."

"Perfectly, Monsieur?"

"Perfectly. Aside from the whole rampaging and instilling terror thing, it performed exactly as designed."

"So you suzpect someone ees behind zis?"

"Someone. Something." He looked off into the distance. "Someplace, perhaps."

"Zomeplace?"

"Let's hope that's not the case. Dr. von Kempelen is looking over his work now. He's been at it since last night. I'm hoping he finds a flaw in the machine."

"You are hoping to find a flaw?"

"That's right. I know that doesn't sound like me. I've never hoped to fail before. But it would be better for the world if this whole incident truly was an industrial accident and not the malicious intent of some mad man."

"What about von Kempelen?" Bertrand asked.

"What about him?"

"Do you zuspect eem? 'E is obviously sneaky and 'as no morals or ezics."

Damian stopped and looked at his longtime friend and companion. "Bertrand, I'm surprised at you. You're not still upset the Val-8 was modeled after you, are you?"

Bertrand's voice jumped up a decibel. "A machine vis my name, dressed een my cloze, vis ma voice eez on ze cover of every papier een ze country!"

Stockwell looked away. "Well, I must say I'm hurt. I thought it was a great compliment. But now I know better, and you don't have to worry. I give you my word that I won't name anything after you ever again."

"Merci."

"Fine." Stockwell continued down the sidewalk. "But, in answer to your question, do I trust the good doctor? I've known this man my entire life. I know him to be financially and ideologically stable. My father fought with him in the war. He's worked for me for a decade. We developed the Val-8 together. He's invited me to his home. I've dined with his family. Two men could not possibly be closer. So yes, I trust him."

"But who else had access to ze machine? Who else could manipulate a device so complicated and unique? And in zuch little time?"

Stockwell considered his friend's words before answering. Bertrand had a point. Most of the robotologists capable of such complex systems had died in recent accidents. Von Kempelen was not only one of the brightest men in his field, he was also one of the last. He hated to admit it, but logic would dictate that he was a suspect. "Trust is a very fluid thing. It kind of comes and goes."

The sentimental part of him had wanted to dismiss von Kempelen's possible involvement. But his rational side had insisted that he consider every angle. Von Kempelen was a family friend who had earned both his loyalty and his father's, and it would be hard to look past two generations of trust.

But, once he looked past that trust, there were obvious signs:

The invitations to family dinner had stopped coming. Were there problems with the marriage?

Von Kempelen had passed on several investment suggestions Damian had given him. Were there money issues?

Is that why there were problems with the marriage?

The closer they'd gotten to the unveiling, the more tired the doctor had appeared. Was he dying of some secret illness?

Is that why there were money issues that were causing problems with the marriage?

They stepped through the front door of the laboratory and into a silent room. On his few visits here, it had been filled with the sounds of progress. Tooling machines ran milling parts for the machine. Engineers sat hunched over workbenches assembling the complex mechanisms that would bring it to life. Men in lab coats scratched equations on chalkboards.

Now there was nothing. The lab was empty and still.

Stockwell broke the silence. "Von Kempelen?"

There was no answer from the dark corners of the lab.

They searched the offices first. Damian expected to find his friend asleep on top of research papers, exhausted from the search for an answer. But the offices were as still as the work area.

"Johan?"

Where was he? Had he run off? Was he trying to flee the country? The questions were piling up and doubt in the good doctor was beginning to rise. Everything now pointed to him, and there was only one way to know for sure that his old friend could be trusted.

They found the doctor in the warehouse inside a hydraulic press, very flat, and very much dead.

"Mon Dieu. Crushed like une pancrepe," Bertrand said.

Stockwell was too overcome to correct his servant. "This is such a relief."

"What?" asked the Frenchman.

"Well, now I know that I can trust him," Stockwell explained.

"Ze man ees dead!"

"Right. So, it also means he probably wasn't dying of some

secret illness. And I'm relieved to hear that."

"How can you be saying zis, Monsieur?"

"But it still doesn't explain why he hasn't invited me to dinner." Stockwell rubbed his chin. "Interesting."

"Monsieur! Ze man has been murdered!"

"Well, thank you, Detective Dupin. Of course he's been murdered." Stockwell gestured to the giant press. "He didn't crawl in there himself and then think, 'hmm, I wonder what this button does?' He knows what that button does, Bertrand! He's a scientist."

Bertrand sputtered the start of several French words before he landed on saying nothing at all.

"This means he wasn't the one who made the Val-8 run amok. This means ..." A smile spread across his face. "This means there is another evil out there."

"'ow can you be zo happy?"

"Because it means I didn't screw this up. Evil did." He put a fist into his palm. "And evil can be dealt with."

"You zaid you wanted to be ze failure."

"I did say that. You're right. But I think it's pretty clear to both of us now that I didn't mean it."

Bertrand threw up his hands and walked into the office to contact the authorities.

Damian picked up a phone in the workshop and made other arrangements.

8

Gremlins in Greenwich

When occupied with a problem, it was not uncommon for Damian to disappear into his lab for days on end. Once locked in a struggle with a problem, the man's magnificent mind could focus on little else. Time meant nothing. Hours, days and minutes became interchangeable. Food became an afterthought. He would emerge only to eat, and only when his stomach was loud enough to become a distraction.

He even slept in his lab. A rollaway cot served as a crash pad for twenty-minute naps that Stockwell claimed could carry him for twelve hours each, especially if several were taken in a row.

There was no use arguing or pleading with him when he was in this state. All calls went unheard. Only the direst of emergencies would pull him from his work. Anything else was a waste of his time.

Bertrand had learned long ago that during these times of

intense focus and thought, it was best to take a vacation and enjoy the quiet time in between the clue and inevitable lead. He never pushed. He knew he would be called when he was needed. He would be called when the lead was discovered. And there would be little rest after that.

A week had passed before he got the call. This was longer than the usual think session, and it had entered Bertrand's thoughts to maybe consider becoming concerned. But before he could really find the time to worry, the call had come, and now he walked down the sidewalk to Stockwell's brownstone home, dreading the condition of the interior.

Damian's devotion to a problem was without compare. He was meticulous in his ponderings and thorough in his considerations. His devotion to housekeeping was another matter, and there would be an awful lot of work to do.

Bertrand walked up the stairs and reached into his pocket for his key. The work would begin inside the door. He expected a pile of mail to impede its opening. It would need to be sorted. Fan letters from children, fan letters from adults, and fan letters and appearance requests from government officials usually made up the bulk of the daily drop. These went into a basket to be addressed when time allowed.

Love letters and promises of devotion got their own basket and would be handled with much more discretion. A delicate balance was needed when breaking a heart.

There was a third basket for licensing requests. Damian's adventures stirred the imagination and companies were eager to latch on to his popularity. Damian had turned down cereal companies, soap manufacturers and tobacco growers with such regularity that one would assume the letters would eventually slow. But the more evil he defeated and the more good Damian did, the larger the stack grew.

The most persistent of all was a young artist named Raymond. His letters stated that he worked as an assistant illustrator, but was looking to make a name for himself with his own comic strip. The young artist pleaded for permission to adapt Stockwell's adventures for syndication. His backup plan was some sort of space adventure that, the artist said, could never compare to the action and heroics of Stockwell's life.

But Stockwell held firm on his policy to never license his image. He knew his exploits would appeal to children, and he feared that they would get hurt in any attempt to emulate his actions. He hoped the young artist and the others would understand this. In their latest exchange, Damian had written that Alex should pursue his secondary option and even suggested a name for the artist to use: Dash Jordon.

Overall, a week's worth of uncollected letters would make for quite a stack.

Bertrand found his key but had not yet removed it from his pocket when he heard the dead bolt slide back and the door begin to open. When he looked up, he was eye to eye with himself. Again. The Frenchman jumped back with a start and kicked his other self in the face. The savateur's strike was powerful—it had felled giants in the past. But now it had little effect as it struck his doppelganger. There was a sharp crack, but no movement from the Val-8 as the face fell from its head and dropped to the ground.

Bertrand pulled his leg back and bounced away to the edge of the landing, giving him room to strike again.

The robot made no move to attack. It bent slowly at the knees, picked up its face and stood in the door frame examining Bertrand with its mechanical eyes. The lenses whirred back and forth for a moment—perhaps adjusting for the lack of a face, perhaps trying to identify the man before him.

The machine made no attempt to reattach its face but merely held it in its hand as it stepped aside and gestured for Bertrand to enter by sweeping an arm towards the foyer.

The Frenchman raised his fists but the robot only repeated the motion. Bertrand let his hands drop to his sides and edged carefully past the machine. There was no pile of letters behind the door.

Bertrand refused to turn his back on the Val-8, and he circled around as the robot shut the door. It turned away and engaged the lock. It then began to climb the steps to the home's second story. It climbed halfway up the staircase and stopped.

Bertrand looked around for anything to use as a weapon. The coatrack was nearby and with a few good shakes it would lose the hats and be an effective staff. But the Val-8 only waved for the valet to follow it up the stairs.

Bertrand followed slowly. He put his hand on the banister, preparing to jump to the ground below if the robot's demeanor changed from friendly to murderous.

The Val-8 turned and proceeded up the staircase at an even pace. Reaching the landing, it turned and waved to Bertrand again.

The valet pulled his hand off the banister. He rubbed his fingers together and noted that the handrail was free of dust. "Merde," he said and moved up the flight.

The Val-8 gently rapped on the door of Stockwell's private lab. The steel door was designed for security and safety, and it rang as the robot's metal knuckles bounced off of it.

Stockwell's voice was muffled behind the thick metal door. There wasn't a trace of fatigue. "Enter."

Bertrand grabbed the knob before the machine could reach for it and let himself into the room. He expected to see a disaster of papers, wires and various other scientific measures strewn about. The room was impeccable. Damian sat in an armchair by an open window sipping a cup of coffee and reading the daily paper.

"Bertrand, my friend. It's good to see you."

The Val-8 crossed the room and handed Stockwell its face.

"What happened to your face?" Damian stood and placed the face back on the machine as it pointed to Bertrand. Damian looked at his valet. "You savated his face off. Didn't you?"

The valet draped his coat on a hook by the door and pointed back at the Val-8. "What is zis?"

"What do you mean? This is the Val-8. You know that."

"You rebuilt it?"

"Of course I rebuilt it. It was the only way to find out what was wrong with it."

"You zaid you would never do zis again. My face. My cloze."

Stockwell laughed. "Oh, I can see your confusion. You think I made another The Bertrand. Well, you're wrong, my friend." He secured the face and the machine set about cleaning the room. "I am a man of my word, and I promised I would never name a miracle of modern science after you again."

Oftentimes when angered by his boss, which was often, Bertrand had difficulty finding the English words best suited to the situations. He knew exactly what he wanted to say; he knew the emotional root of the conversation, but the kind and less profane equivalents escaped him. In cases like this he usually ended up making his frustration known with hand gestures.

He frantically pointed to the robot several times.

"This is not The Bertrand," Stockwell said. "This is The Bertron."

"Ze Bertron?!"

"Yes, The Bertron."

"How ees zat any different?"

"Spelling, for one. Also it was available as a trademark. And I should thank you for being offended, because the new name sounds so much more 'man of tomorrow.' The marketing team thinks it will sell an extra thousand units alone."

"You are still planning on zelling eet?"

"Of course. The world needs this." Stockwell moved across the room to a surprisingly ordered workbench and picked up a small black object.

"What eef eet goes berserk again?"

"It can't." Stockwell tossed the item across the room.

Bertrand's reflexes kicked in and he snagged the box out of the air.

Stockwell pointed to the device. "Not without that."

Bertrand turned the item over in his hands. It was nothing

but a small black metal box. It was no larger than three inches each way. He held it to his ear and it made no sound.

"What eez eet?"

"That, my friend, is a gremlin."

"A gremlin? Zis?"

"I know. I thought they'd be green, too. But that's the device that caused all the excitement at the fair. That is what sullied my good name and set the future back."

Bertrand shook the device again. "Zo why did eet not work?"

Stockwell smiled. "It worked beautifully. Whoever put it in the Val-8 sure knew what they were doing."

"Zis eez not yours?"

"Of course not. The Val-8 was designed to be autonomous. That is a radio transceiver. Do you know what that means?"

Bertrand tossed the device back on the workbench. "Non."

"It means someone sabotaged the machine. It means that someone was nearby controlling it. It means someone wanted the Val-8 to run amok at the fair. And, most importantly, it means it wasn't my fault."

Bertrand pointed to the Val-8 as it tidied the room. "But now you're just going to leave eet on."

"Sure, why not? It's doing a great job around here."

Bertrand crossed the room and stood next to The Bertron. "What eef eet happeens zageen? What eef someone takes ze control and eet kills someone?"

"It can't. Watch." Stockwell turned towards the robot valet. "The Bertron, come here and bend down."

The machine complied and Damian grabbed it by the hair. He pulled the wig from its head, revealing a wire mesh. "I've shielded it from all radio waves. Even if someone could plant the device again, they wouldn't be able to talk to it."

"Destroy eet."

"Don't be silly, my friend. It's not going to cause any more problems." He placed the wig back on the robot, then looked at the machine and the Frenchman standing next to it. "Except …"

"Exzept what?"

"I'm going to have a hard time telling the two of you apart." Stockwell laughed and slapped Bertrand on the shoulder. "Maybe you should wear a hat."

"Zis ees unacceptable."

"He's handy."

"'andy? Bah! What can ee do zat I cannot?"

Stockwell went back to the workbench and looked at the device. "Don't be that way, Bertrand. Come here."

The Bertron responded immediately to the command. Bertrand sat in the chair with a huff and crossed his arms.

Damian turned and put his hands on the robot's shoulders. "Don't worry, my friend. A machine could never replace you."

"I am over eere."

Stockwell turned, "Oh."

"Maybe ee needs ze 'at."

"We don't have time for your petty jealousy, Bertrand. We have to find out where this device came from. And, more importantly, who was controlling The Bertrand when it terrified the midway."

"Maybe eet was ze doctor."

Stockwell grew a crooked smile. "The dead doctor?"

"Ee wasn't dead zen."

"Interesting. Though I'm pretty sure he was cleared of any wrongdoing the moment he was shoved into the press and squeezed to death."

"Maybe zere were more conspirators and zey were covering zeir tracks."

"I hate to think of von Kempelen that way," Damian said. "But it may be worth considering. We'll have plenty of time to think about it on our way to London."

"London?"

"Of course. President Roosevelt has asked me to address the London Economic Conference. I told you all about it."

Bertrand shook his head.

The Bertron pointed a thumb towards itself. "Oh, I knew I told one of you about it."
Bertrand put his face in his hands. "Merde."

9

Conference of Concern

Since the dawn of time, man had studied rock. Some scientists theorized that rocks may have been the very first thing ever studied. They claimed that when the first man walked out of his cave and stepped on a sharp rock, his thoughts would have been, "Ouch, what was that upon which I stepped?" He would then have picked it up, examined the object and determined that it was a rock.

Unless it was a stick. But it was probably a rock.

The Geological Museum in London was dedicated to the study of the things beneath man's feet. Having moved far beyond the sharp rock outside the cave, the museum collected and studied many other types of rocks and their place in the world.

Gold was one such rock.

This must have been the reason the museum was selected to host the London Economic Forty-Three Conference of 1933. The building was nice enough. The stone pillars gave it an academic feel that would befit such a conference, but Damian couldn't help but feel there could be a more exciting location chosen instead of a building filled with rocks.

It didn't really matter. It wasn't his place to question the site. He was there at the behest of his president to join with sixty-six other nations to fight global depression.

Of course, he had jumped at the opportunity. Through the course of his adventures, he had fought many things. These travails were well documented by a press that always had to add its own colorful flair. He had fought the "Despot of Danzig," "The Butcher of Botswana," and the "The Sickly Saint of San Marino." He had defeated the "Demon of Dominica," "The Howling Horror of Hawaii," and "The Broken Bastard Beast of Bolivia." He had fought and defeated men and monsters all over the world, but he had never fought global depression, and he looked forward to the challenge.

He began to wonder what the press would call it. "Damian Stockwell and the Economy of Evil?" "Damian Stockwell and the Rancid Recession?" "Damian Stockwell and the Depression of Doom?" He smirked at the thought; they had such an attraction to alliteration.

Like any great story, the situation was rife with conflict. The world wanted to weaken the dollar through currency stabilization. They believed that this settlement would relieve the world of the crushing debt burdens many nations faced after the war. The president was against the idea as it was the United States that the world owed. Stockwell was against a weaker dollar due to the mere fact that if a depression needed to be fought, it was better to have something stronger than something weaker.

As a personal request, the president asked Damian to speak at the conference and inspire the world to pull itself up by the bootstraps and work its way out of the depression instead of welching on debts owed to America. Stockwell had never refused a president, and he wasn't about to start now.

After a brief introduction, he made his way up to the dais and looked out over the crowd. He cleared his throat and began to speak. "Good afternoon. My name is Damian Stockwell, of America, and I want to talk to you about a dream."

A bevy of translators spoke after him, turning his words into French, German, Russian and many other languages. Hearing the world unite behind his words made him smile. He allowed the translations to trail off before continuing.

"It's a dream I like to call Liberty. Now, this isn't the kind of dream that your wife tries to tell you about and you just zone out and nod along. This isn't the kind of dream Freud would ask you to talk about and then twist your words around until he made it seem like you're attracted to your mother ... or your mother's sister ... or the maid ... or, seriously what is wrong with that guy? I mean, everything is genitalia to him. Everything but his cigar—which I find more than a little convenient.

"No, this is a dream about freedom. Freedom from poverty. Freedom from depression, both economic and emotional. It's freedom from the idea that one must be weakened to make another stronger and other silly concepts.

"This dream is real, and it's happening every day in a place I like to call America."

The translators chattered away. His words sounded so poetic in French and Russian. They sounded phlegmy in German. He spoke most of these languages, but to hear them all spoken at once reminded him how small the world really was. Almost every language shared a common root and all of mankind shared a history that, fight as they may, they could never escape. We are united in our past. We are brothers in history and family in the struggle for progress, and at no time was this more evident than when each translator got to the word genitalia.

It made Damian smile.

"All across my country people aren't just looking to manipulate wealth through fuzzy math or by kicking the chair out from under someone else. They're creating it.

"They're creating it through hard work, discipline, dedication and, most of all, science." He looked beyond the crowd to a display of rocks and sneered.

"Real science. All over the world there are sciences happening that don't just study rocks. These are useful sciences and they're creating breakthroughs. And every breakthrough is an opportunity. An opportunity to find liberty."

He paused for effect and to let the translators catch up. When they finished, he paused longer so their pause would have the same effect as his initial pause. It would seem easy to translate a pause, but there was an art to it, and Stockwell held the brush.

"Just last month a scientist by the name of Karl Jansky made a discovery that will change not only our world, but worlds beyond our own." Stockwell had read the paper on Jansky's discovery only once. Once was enough to recall every minute detail, but he knew that too much minutia would lose the audience.

Jansky's findings were monumental and pioneered a field the man had called radio astronomy, but Damian decided to cut to the chase. "Deep within the center of our own galaxy, Dr. Jansky," Jansky was not technically a doctor, but he knew the title would play well to the crowd, "detected radio waves of extra-terrestrial origin."

He felt a general disbelief roll through the crowd and he couldn't blame them. Jansky's finding wasn't made of rock, so even the scientists at the museum had missed the news.

"That's right, ladies and gentlemen. Dr. Jansky has discovered what can only be called alien radio waves, and I think you can see what this means.

"This opens up a whole new market for all of us. Gone are the days of us trading only with other nations. Human-to-human marketing is the old way. The new Silk Road is being blazed through outer space to a planet in the constellation Sagittarius.

"Some of the world's greatest minds have already met on this and pondered the possibilities. These brilliant minds have determined that the Sagittarians have a massive amount of disposable income since it is obvious that they don't have to spend it all on pants or footwear. That's a lot of discretionary spending, my friends."

Several translators looked at him. They looked lost. Perhaps they were searching for their language's word for Sagittarians. Stockwell covered the mic and tried to help them. Once they had caught up, he continued.

"This is the dream I'm talking about. Through science we have not only discovered a new consumer group, we've discovered how to communicate with them.

"As we speak, my broadcasting company, BroadDam, is hard at work developing programming for our new galactic neighbors, and in just a few short months we will begin beaming entertainment to our four-legged listeners.

"Obviously we're starting with westerns. We believe these oaters will be twice as popular with our new Centaurian brothers and sisters as they are with us.

"But our dream doesn't stop there. We're working on a science fiction serial called *Gallop Across the Stars*, a mystery series called *Four Feet From Murder,* and a comedy called *Why the Long Face?*"

The humor went over the heads of those in the crowd, but that was to be expected. It was Centaurian humor, and the writers had assured him it would make them whinny all the way to the cash register.

"Interstellar commerce is just one new field, just one weapon in our fight against global depression. Science will provide more weapons and with them we will prevail."

The translators finished conveying his words and the crowd did not applaud. They only stared at him. He was not surprised. He had just opened their minds to a whole new world. They would see the hope in his message soon, but it was too much to ask for instantaneous understanding. Stockwell smiled and leaned closer to the microphone.

"We will fight this global depression, not by arbitrarily

affixing a value to paper, but through science. Real science. And that is my dream. Thank you."

He smiled and waved to the audience as he stepped away from the podium. The US Secretary of State, Cordell Hull, stood at the foot of the riser with a blank expression, shaking his head.

Stockwell realized at once what he had done. The secretary was next in line to speak and Damian had kept his notes a secret. "My apologies, Mr. Hull. I'd hate to follow that as well." He put his hand on the secretary's shoulder. "But I'm sure you'll do fine."

10

Myself, My Enemy

The interior of the Dorchester was decorated in an optimism that the oncoming global strife would never phase. In only two years, the hotel had secured its reputation and a clientele that would see an economic depression as nothing more than a slight setback.

It was appointed with the finest furnishings of the day and made no pretenses to be anything but the finest hotel in London. Richly paneled Georgian mahogany doors welcomed the guests, and inside the lavishly appointed lobby a host of stewards waited to point out the richly paneled Georgian mahogany doors. Gold leaf and marble ran throughout the hotel in attempt to draw the visitors back to the gilded age.

He had spent the remainder of the day at the conference listening to other speeches much less invigorating than his and feigning interest.

The majority of the attendants were pushing for a

devaluation of the US dollar and a weakening of America, and Stockwell was forced to smile through these affronts. It was tiring holding his tongue, but not as tiring as holding his fists as one speaker after another made blaming America the center of their platform.

They blamed his country for being greedy. They blamed his country for exploiting the world. They blamed America for everything and demanded that the nation forgive their debts, and they didn't even say please. Not once.

It had taken every bit of him to not give them a piece of his mind, and now he stepped into his hotel room with a heavy sigh, wanting nothing more than to relax. He collapsed onto a chesterfield before draping an arm across his eyes. Tomorrow would be more of the same.

Bertrand closed the door to the suite. The valet had mingled with the crowd and reported the same attitude from the others. It seemed the entire world had decided the best way to stimulate the global economy was to avoid paying their debts to the United States.

The frustration had been too much for Damian, so they had spent the ride to the hotel discussing the Val-8's sabotage instead. Pitting his mind against a sinister plot often calmed his nerves.

Further examination of the device inside the machine had revealed few actual clues. Normally the design alone would reveal the signature of the designer. Engineers had their quirks like anyone else, and these trademarks often showed through in their designs. But the black box was something different. Its design was brutally efficient. No space was wasted. No solder overdone. And it was so advanced that Damian knew of no engineer capable of such work. The power supply alone put it into the realm of scientific breakthrough.

The as yet unknown villain's lack of a motive was even more frustrating. DamIndustries had no shortage of competitors that would delight in his downfall and revel in his humiliation. These companies were ruthless enough, but none were capable of such technology. The rampage was meant to do more than give his reputation a black eye. The dead robotologist was proof enough of that.

This led him down another path of thought. What of the other robotologists' deaths of late? As events unfolded, each accidental death was beginning to look more like murder. Each had died, in one form or another, at the hands of their own creations with little explanation for the tragic turn but, "Meh, robot."

Stockwell tired of sitting on the chesterfield. Why did everything here have to be so different? What he wouldn't give for a good old-fashioned American couch. He had inquired at the desk, but they had only given him blank stares in return. "Bertrand. Draw me a bath. As hot as you can make it."

"Oui, Monsieur."

Cold showers were the best way to begin any day, but a hot bath did more to soothe physical and mental anguish. He heard the Frenchman turn on the water, and a moment later steam drifted from the bathroom.

It was time to focus on other problems. The distraction would do him good. Thoughts of villains that were mysterious saboteurs and global depression would continue in the back of his mind, but he needed something else to focus on. He had requested a radio in the bathroom for just this reason.

He called to Bertrand, "And turn on the news."

The compact model had been in storage for some time. He imagined the smell of the dust warming on the tubes as the volume built. He heard the valet fumble the dial until the familiar, soothing cadence of a BBC reporter could be heard beyond the running water. It didn't matter what they were reporting: local color or global disaster, the broadcasters treated every story with a calm professionalism that Stockwell appreciated. When absorbing information, it should remain free of emotion. Emotion only muddled facts with feelings.

A hot bath. A mental distraction. All he needed now was a drink. He stood and walked to the bar cart as Bertrand stepped back into the room. "Your baz ees drawing."

"Thank you, Bertrand. That will be all for today. I'll call you in the morning when I can summon the patience to return to the conference."

"Merci, Monsieur." The valet turned to leave but was stopped by a sharp rap at the suite door.

Stockwell rolled his steel gray eyes. He was in no mood for visitors. Silence and whiskey were the only company he desired. "Tell them I'm in the bath!"

Bertrand nodded and moved to the door. He leaned against it and spoke through the wood, "Our apologies. We are een ze baz."

"I'm in the bath!" Stockwell corrected him as he slammed down the rocks glass hard enough to jettison a piece of ice. "You really need to work on your pronouns, Bertrand."

"My apologies, Monsieur." He turned back to the door. "I'm een ze bath."

Damian was about to correct his servant again, but he figured it would do no good. As long as the visitor went away, he didn't care who was in the bath.

But the visitor wasn't buying the bath story. His voice came through the door loud and clear. "Mr. Stockwell. It's the president. We need to speak."

"The president?" Stockwell turned from the bar cart. "What's he doing here?"

"Eet doezn't sound like ze prezident," Bertrand said.

"It sounds exactly like the president."

"Eet doze not."

"Of course it does. Listen." Stockwell coughed, sat down and put on his best Roosevelt impression. "Mr. Stockwell, it's the president." Damian resumed his normal baritone. "See?"

"That doezn't zound like ze prezident eizer."

"It sounds just like that guy." Stockwell pointed to the door.

Bertrand nodded. "Oui. Your prezident and zat prezident zound alike. But neizer zound like ze real prezident."

Stockwell waved it off. "I'm sure it's a language barrier

thing. Bertrand, let the president in."

"But ..."

"But, nothing, Bertrand. Now, please, open the door for our commander in chief." Stockwell stepped to a mirror, straightened his shirt and ran a hand through his hair.

Bertrand opened the door, laughed out loud and closed it without letting the visitor enter.

Damian turned back to the door. "Why didn't you let him in?"

Bertrand could not hide the amusement. "Eet eez not ze prezident."

"Well, who is it?"

The Frenchman laughed again and stepped away from the door. "Karma?"

The suite door exploded in a storm of splinters and Damian Stockwell stepped into the suite.

Damian leapt back and he came face-to-face with himself. The physique was perfect. Its posture—impeccable. The hair was an exact match right down to the part. And the face—the face was beautiful. It wasn't plastic like The Bertron's. The skin was blemish free, the tone was a perfect match, and when the man before him smiled the proper creases and dimples appeared. If he hadn't have been Damian Stockwell, he would have sworn upon a bible in a court of law that he was staring at Damian Stockwell. "What the hell is this?"

"Maybe hiz name eez Ze Damion," Bertrand laughed.

"That's not funny, Bertrand."

"That's not funny, Bertrand," the new Damian repeated the words, matching the tone, the inflection and the amount of hurt in Stockwell's voice.

"What eez eet doing?" asked Bertrand.

"I don't know."

"I don't know," the doppelganger repeated.

Damian pointed at the machine. "It's copying me!"

The machine pointed back. "It's copying me!"

"Stop copying me, imposter!"

"Stop copying me, imposter!"

Damian turned to his valet. "Bertrand, tell him to stop copying me."

The counterfeit Damian turned to the Frenchman. "Bertrand, tell him to stop copying me."

"Uh, pleeze stop repeating eem? One eez truly enough."

The intruder said nothing.

Stockwell folded his arms across his chest and said, "That's more like it."

The intruder did the same.

"Okay, I have had enough of this."

The intruder repeated the statement, but most of the speech was lost in a whiskey bottle that broke across his face. The imposter didn't flinch. It didn't move at all. The broken glass had cut the skin, and blood seeped from the gashes, but the man before them didn't react at all.

Damian shook his head. "I hated to do that. That was good whiskey." He laughed his contagious laugh and stopped only when the doppelganger began to copy him.

The mimic laughed and then spoke its own words for the first time. "Library complete. You cannot stop us, Mr. Stockwell. We are everywhere."

Stockwell looked at the bottle's neck in his hand. He tipped it over and spilled what was left onto the floor.

The machine spoke again. "We've fixed the flaws in your pathetic design. Water cannot stop us. You cannot stop us. We are now unstoppable."

Damian dropped the broken bottleneck and fell into a defensive stance. He had created the martial art of Damitsu to be a system as fluid as any situation, but he had never before faced himself. How much did this machine know about him? Could it predict his movements? Would it know what he was thinking? There was no way to tell. And he wasn't about to wait to find out.

Stockwell leapt forward. His right foot snapped forward at

the point of impact and collided with the robot's chest. It was like jumping into a wall. He sprang back and marveled at how well they had duplicated his physical stature.

Bertrand's foot flew from the ground and connected with the machine's face. There was a thwack of shoe leather hitting skin, but the machine did not groan or cry out.

The Frenchman bounced back with a smile on his face.

"Quit enjoying this."

"I am zorry, Monsieur," he said, but the smile held.

"No you're not."

"I am zorry, but I am not."

"We'll talk about this later, Bertrand."

The imposter lunged forward with both arms outstretched, attempting to ensnare both men. Each ducked away to a separate side of the room. They had fought together many times, and coordinating their efforts had long since passed into instinct. But this was something new.

"What should we do?" Bertrand asked.

"I don't know," Stockwell said. "Hit it with a car?"

Bertrand connected a vicious foot to the back of the machine's head as it passed by and sent it tumbling forward.

As it fell, the machine swung wide with its left arm and caught Stockwell in the chest. The blow sent him across the room and he sank deep into the plush coverings on the bed.

The Damian caught its balance before it hit the ground. It stood and turned to look at Stockwell. "Mere punches cannot defeat me. I am mighty."

"I will zay, ee zounds juzt like you." Bertrand threw a lamp at its head. It shattered and made a mess on the floor but had no effect, other than adding a line item to the hotel bill.

Stockwell reached under the pillow and pulled out his .45 automatic. He looked down the barrel and stared at his own face in the iron sights. Practiced tendons in his finger pulled the trigger to the absolute brink of releasing the firing pin. He stopped there. "Please don't make me do this."

The machine marched forward.

Through his adventures, he had never faced a more psychologically devious opponent. How was one supposed to remain objective as he stared into his own eyes? How could he fire upon himself without some part of his psyche suffering injury?

Stockwell closed his eyes as he fired at himself, hoping it would be enough to spare him emotional scarring. He felt every slug that tore into The Damian's perfectly sculpted chest.

The rounds had no effect.

The Damian, bleeding from every wound in its body, leaned over and grabbed Stockwell by the throat and lifted him into the air. "You're obsolete, human. We'll take it from here."

Stockwell pulled against the steel fingers of the machine. "Hardly. Your library is incomplete."

The fingers squeezed harder. "All required records have been stored."

"Not quite." Stockwell's voice faded. "You've never heard me scream."

The fingers froze and Stockwell saw a quick flash behind his own piercing steel blue eyes.

The machine spoke again. "Scream for us, Damian Stockwell."

"My pleasure." Damian opened his mouth to its fullest extent and screamed. His powerful lungs bellowed a note fit for an opera house. It carried through the room and rattled the glasses on the bar cart. He finished the note and smiled.

The machine opened its mouth to repeat the sound.

Stockwell reached into his pocket and pulled out the tiny black transceiver. He smiled as he shoved it deep into the robot's mouth.

The Damian tried to imitate the scream, but the even cadence of the BBC was the only sound that escaped its mouth. The machine looked confused as it struggled to find its voice.

"Bertrand," Stockwell wheezed against the grip. "Music, please."

"Oui, Monsieur." The valet rushed into the bathroom.

Bursts of static filled The Damian's speech in between segments of conversations as Bertrand spun through the radio's dial.

The machine dropped Damian and tore at its mouth, trying to get at the transceiver between bursts of programming. Once Bertrand found a waltz on the radio, however, the machine stopped grasping and began dancing. It lumbered around the room with an imaginary partner, spinning and twirling as it went.

Damian smiled and climbed off the bed. "Look, Bertrand, they've even copied my dance moves."

"Oui, I zee. 'E eez terreeble."

"Just for that, you lead."

Bertrand hung his head and mumbled, "Oui, Monsieur." The valet walked across the room and cut in on the imaginary dance partner. He took The Damian by the hand and began to lead the robot in the waltz. Bertrand sighed. "Where to?"

"Into the tub, of course."

Bertrand spun once and moved the robot towards the bathroom. It took two more measures to get it inside the door. As the final notes sounded, he backed the machine up against the tub and pushed it in.

The splash was substantial and the robot's body clanged as it hit the steel tub. Its face hit the edge and the transceiver dropped from its mouth to the floor.

Stockwell picked it up and placed it in his pocket as The Damian calculated its new surroundings. It began to laugh Stockwell's infectious laugh. "I told you we are now waterproof. We are impervious. We are unstoppable."

Damian slid the radio from the shelf above the tub. It fell with a splash into the claw foot basin. The warbled sounds of the next movement began as sparks filled the water.

The robot's limbs reacted to the disturbance in a very human manner, flopping and jiggling, turning the water into froth. This went on for a few moments as transistors burned out and relays quit firing. When it was over, it looked like Damian Stockwell had died in the tub.

Bertrand smiled.

Stockwell looked at his dead, smoking self, then turned away and left the room.

11

Locked Away

The Bertron answered the door without his face. The mechanical eyes whirred and scanned Bertrand beyond the shopping bags for only a moment before letting him in.

Bertrand handed the machine the bags and watched as it dutifully took them to the kitchen and began to put the contents away. The valet moved up the staircase towards Stockwell's second-floor parlor and found it empty. His friend and employer normally took breakfast in this room. Nothing had been normal since London.

The world's greatest adventurer had not been seen in several days. Bertrand had been turned away at the door several times by that damned machine. It wasn't until that morning that he had finally received a call and was allowed into the home.

It wasn't unusual for Damian to disappear into his lab, but after the encounter with his doppelganger, his friend had been more shaken than Bertrand had ever seen him.

The man's composure and resiliency was legendary, and even under the most stressful situations it was hard to detect the shaken nerves of the great man. But Bertrand knew him better than almost anyone, and he could spot the signs of his flustered nature. Damian had been testy, to say the least. Every little thing had bothered him on the flight home. He yelled at Bertrand several times without seeking forgiveness. He yelled at the weather and the gauges on the plane. And when he wasn't snapping at someone or something, he was completely silent. He offered nothing, not even manners, to those they encountered.

Stockwell watched everyone with a wary eye. He was a master at observing without calling attention to himself, but now he did not even try to hide his suspicions. He wanted everyone to know they were being watched and scrutinized. Even Bertrand fell under the suspicious gaze.

Coming face to face with, and then being forced to electrocute, himself had been jarring to say the least. Once they landed, Stockwell ordered the inoperable machine to his lab and told Bertrand to give him space to think. Those were the last words he'd heard from his friend and employer until the call came this morning.

Bertrand dropped the morning paper on the small café table by the parlor window and stepped back into the hallway. He crossed the hallway to the lab and knocked on the door.

The only response was a brisk and cold, "Enter."

Bertrand turned the knob and slowly opened the door.

The lab was a mess. Not untidy, but unorganized. Strewn with wires and cables, the room appeared set upon by a mechanical spider. Dials and meters pinged and beeped from every direction. Machines of all kinds were wired together and stacked on top of one another. The whole room hummed. Bertrand had never seen it like this.

"Come in, Bertrand." Stockwell's voice could be measured against the mechanical pulse of the room.

"Monsieur? Are you okay?" he asked.

"I'm fine, Bertrand." Stockwell finished the statement with a long glance.

"I waz worried about you after what 'appened in London."

"I'll be honest with you, my friend. London left me shaken. No man should ever be forced to kill himself."

"I underztand ze feeling."

"But that's not what has me disturbed."

"What eez eet zen?"

"It's a question of trust, Bertrand. Who can I trust, if I can't trust myself? If they—whoever they may be—can perfectly replicate me, they could replicate anyone. If I could be a robot, anyone could be a robot."

The giant man paused for a moment and straightened up to his full height.

"You could be a robot."

"I assure you, Monsieur, I am not un robot."

"I believe you, my friend. I do. But you'll understand if I don't. Because 'I am not a robot' is exactly what a robot would say." Damian turned and walked farther into the lab. He had to duck under some of the new equipment as he made his way. "I have to be certain, and that's why I've locked myself away in the lab for the last few days. I had to find a foolproof way to test for humanity."

He arrived at a chair in the corner of the room and turned it to face the valet. It squeaked its protest. "Won't you help me? My friend?"

"Don't be zilly, of course—"

"I'm not being silly. If you are who you say you are, this won't be a problem. Come here, Bertrand." He patted the chair and stepped over to a bank of machines.

Bertrand made his way through the lab. He had to duck under the wires and step over cables as he went. Everything hummed with electricity, and the stacks of equipment blew warm air on him as he passed. The whole room buzzed and crackled with static and disparate tones. He arrived at the chair.

Stockwell pointed to the seat. "Sit down."

He could see in his friend's eyes that protesting would just prolong the situation. He knew he was no robot and had nothing to fear other than the fact that Stockwell's test might injure, maim or kill him. "Eez eet safe?"

Stockwell stopped playing with the dials on the machine and adopted his most authoritative tone. "I would never endanger a decent human life, and you know it."

Bertrand moved to sit and stopped. "How are you defining dezent?"

"Sit down!"

Bertrand sighed and sat.

Stockwell stepped from behind the machine, leaned over and said, "It's perfectly safe." He then quickly secured both of Bertrand's wrists to the arms of the chair with metal bands.

"What eez zis?!" Bertrand yelled.

"Be still." The man of science stepped back behind the green electrical box and remerged with a pair of thick cables terminating into large jagged-toothed clamps.

"What are you doing?!" Bertrand fought against the clamps, but they held his arms firmly against the arms of the chair.

"The test. It won't take but a moment." Stockwell affixed the clamps to the restrictive bands and backed away.

"What are you going to do?!" Bertrand thrashed against the chair. The wooden legs screamed against the ground and squeaked as he pushed the joints to their limits.

"Stop squirming. You're doing fine. And we're almost done." Stockwell stood up and slapped Bertrand across the face.

Bertrand stopped struggling and stared at his employer. The valet spoke several languages and quickly spewed every swear word, curse and insult he knew—twice—as he tried to break free of the chair's hold.

Damian smiled. "Good. You passed the test. I told you you'd do fine."

"Sacre bleu. Zat waz ze test?!"

"Yes. You see, the machines have quickly adapted to every weakness we've exposed. And we can only expect them to keep on doing so. Any test has to be something they can't prepare against. My hand. It can quickly determine whether or not a metal skeleton lurks beneath the surface of a person's face. No amount of science can hide from my blows."

"Zat's eet? Zen what eez all zis equipment for?"

"Oh, the equipment is from earlier tests. They worked, too, but I'm afraid they would kill anything that was human."

"Why did you strap me down? What about ze clamps?"

Stockwell undid the clamps and turned off the electrical box. "That was to electrocute you in case you were a robot. And I strapped you down because I was going to slap you and I didn't want to get hit. It's one of the side effects of the tests."

"Let me out of zis chair."

"Not so fast, my friend. I have a theory I want to run by you first. And I don't think it would hurt if you calmed down a bit."

Bertrand struggled against them, but the bands held his wrists firm to the chair. He gave up the struggle and asked, "What eez zis seory?"

Damian crossed the room to an object covered by a black cloth. He pulled away the tarp to reveal The Damian sitting upright in a chair. "This machine. It was a little too perfect. Don't you think?"

"How do you mean?"

"It looked like me. It acted like me. And more importantly, it sounded like me. And I don't think that's a coincidence."

Bertrand rolled his eyes, "Eet waz zupposed to be you."

"Exactly. And that is no easy task. You know me better than most people, and I doubt that even you fully understand me. I'm complex, complicated. I'm more than the sum of my parts. And that would be very difficult to duplicate. What I'm saying is, I'm one of a kind."

"Zank God," Bertrand muttered.

"Even to get the very rudimentary and bland personality of the Val-8, we had to study you for weeks."

"Study me?"

"Oh, you know. The standard stuff, film, personality assessments, listening in on your phone calls."

"What?"

"Well, we couldn't just ask you to record something for us. It would sound forced and dishonest. People like honesty, Bertrand. They like genuine."

"You don't zay. What eez your point?"

"My point is that in order to so perfectly impersonate me, it would have taken months of study. Detailed study. Copious notes. Hours of recordings. Endless pictures. And I was thinking that there was only one person that had that kind of close, personal access to me."

Bertrand understood. "Of course. Eet could only be …"

"You. That's right. But now we know that you're not a robot, so I'm back to square one." He cupped his lantern chin in his hand and narrowed his eyes in thought.

"Gah," Bertrand gahed. "Eet waz ze girl! Eet's obviouzly ze girl."

"The girl?" Stockwell repeated. "Which girl?"

"Ze reporter! She spent monthz wiz you. Alwayz wiz 'er notebook. 'er photographair took 'ow many photos of you?"

Damian smiled. "Hundreds?"

"And did she evair record your voize?"

"We met once a week in the studio. She wanted to release a phonographic version of the interview for syndication."

"And for 'ow many people 'ave you done your prezidential imperzonazion?"

"Gah! Bertrand, it was only her."

Bertrand nodded his head to the side.

"She must be working for the villains that are behind this plot."

"Eet would zeem zo. Pleeze let me up."

Stockwell sat heavily on a workbench stool. "I don't want to believe it. Was I so blinded by vanity and flattery that I missed all the clues?"

"Probably. Let me up."

"But you're right. It was the perfect cover to learn my every move, my voice, my hair, my—everything. I feel so betrayed. Do you have any idea what that's like?"

"You strapped me to a chair and you slapped me."

"That's different. It was for our safety. I now know that I can trust you like I always have. It's that woman, Bertrand. We've got to find Angelica Palmer."

Bertrand balled his fists. "I will help. Let me up."

"I have to make a stop first." Stockwell opened the door to the lab. He grabbed his hat from the hook on the wall and turned back to Bertrand. "I'll send The Bertron up to help you out." And with that he was gone.

Bertrand looked around the room and back to his hands. "Merde."

12

Library of Liberty

A true adventurer never sought glory. The only reason they pursued the unknown was to make it known. They dared to shed light on the world around them. They risked everything to expose history to today. And, possibly, they may have occasionally dug into the far reaches of danger to find fortune. But they never did it for glory. It was for this reason that the Vagabond Club's New York chapter was housed in a nondescript building.

Its entrance was not grand. No banner flew announcing its stature as the world's most exclusive private club. No doorman welcomed the elite members as they mounted the stairs. The Vagabond Club was quite extraordinarily plain.

Damian marveled at how appearances could be deceiving. Of course, he had planned for the building to be deceiving, so that didn't surprise him. But on the other hand, the reporter had fooled him in a way no one else ever had. She had appeared to be on the level in every way.

He hadn't just gone on instinct. Though he was an impeccable judge of character, the nature of the Val-8 project had demanded the upmost secrecy. The reporter had been subjected to comprehensive background checks, extensive interviews, and a number of sworn oaths before she had been granted access to Stockwell. She was diabolical.

And not only had she gotten inside his organization, she had gotten him to open up, as well. It was no wonder his robot other was such a perfect match. He had fallen for her story and given her his own. Now he had to find her and get the truth.

Stockwell opened the ordinary doors and stepped into a small, ordinary alcove. There was nothing in the room but a desk and an attendant in a blue uniform. The man rose from his seat but did not seem to get any taller.

"Good evening, Sammy," Stockwell said.

"Mr. Stockwell. It's good to see you. I trust you're having a good day."

"I've had better, Sammy. But it's nothing I can't handle. What about you? How's the missus?"

Sammy shifted from one foot to another. "I'm not married, sir."

"I'm sorry to hear that. What happened?"

"I've never been married, sir. Not a day."

Stockwell looked over at the wall. "Well, I'm sure it's for the best."

"You seem a little distracted today, sir. Maybe I should just let you in."

"Thank you, Sammy. My love to the family."

"I've no family, sir." Sammy reached under the desk and pressed a button. "I'm a very lonely man."

"That's the spirit, Sammy." A wall panel slid open next to Damian, and the founding Vagabond entered his club.

Beyond the tiny alcove, the entrance to the club reached several stories. Every inch of the massive expanse was covered with murals depicting the great adventurers of myth and legend.

Stockwell stopped in the center of the room and stood on the Vagabond crest between the expansive wings of a soaring eagle. He read the words on the crest aloud. "Vagus, calleo, recurs. Amen." He looked at the mural to his right. Achilles was dying. An arrow stuck in his heel and his blood ran into the sand. The world's mightiest warrior was brought down not by courage or might or even the fates, but by a secret and a sniveling coward who fired from the darkness. It was not an honorable death. It was less than a man so mighty deserved.

Stockwell nodded to the painting. "I know the feeling, brother." He sighed and moved on through the atrium into the grand hall.

The decor here did not suffer from the immaturity of the Chicago chapter. Every room of the New York clubhouse smelled of age and adventure. Every piece of furniture and décor had a history. Every piece was contributed by a formal member of the club as a testament to their adventures around the globe.

Most of the pieces were antiques. Many were blessed. Others were cursed. All of it was unique. One chair was haunted by a particularly nasty Aztec king that didn't appreciate anyone sitting in his seat. Members of the club often offered it to new members as an informal form of hazing. They always got a good laugh when Tizoc made his presence known and chased the rookie around the room with a maquahuitl.

The club's lounge smelled of brandy, cigars and plotting, and members filled the seats. While some appeared to relax, it was unlike a Vagabond to sit completely idle. Many pored over ancient texts or modern day charts. They were either on the trail of some great mystery or looking for the trail itself.

Stockwell waved to several members as he passed through the lounge and made his way towards the outfitter's shop. Membership in the club came with many benefits, not the least of which was access to Cam Williams, the Vagabond outfitter.

Chasing down the world's great discoveries often required

specialized equipment designed specifically for the field of operations. Buying off the shelf was rarely an option for a great expedition, and Williams was a genius engineer who could deliver brilliance in almost any form. There wasn't a problem he couldn't outthink or a challenge he couldn't out-design.

His shop occupied the back half of the club and, even though genius tended to get a little messy and occasionally explode, it was one of Damian's favorite places.

Real work was done here. Men worked with their hands and pitted their dexterity and brute strength against the elements of nature, bending and shaping them to their will. Men toiled at their crafts all around him. Electricians worked from diagrams and chalkboards to produce all manner of devices that chirped and warbled. Carpenters turned wood into an earthy aroma as they cut, carved and crafted the pieces to shape. Metalworkers lent mood to the room with their arc welders. Cracks of blue escaped the workshop and split the air to create the distinct scent of ozone. It always smelled like spring in the Vagabond workshop.

Stockwell found Williams behind a bouquet of flowers, holding the office phone receiver loosely between his ear and shoulder with a look of pained disinterest on his face. The man was short but built thick and more than a little annoyed at the caller on the other end of the line.

"Well, maybe I wouldn't mind the ocean being a little closer to my house. What do you think of that?" He slammed down the receiver before noticing his guest. "Oh, hey, Dam."

Damian stepped up to the desk and pointed at the phone. "What was that all about?"

Williams pulled a greasy rag from his back pocket and began to wipe his hands. It was a nervous habit Stockwell had noticed in the man for some time. This move put more grease on his hands than anything else.

The outfitter shrugged. "Some lunatic says there's a planet or two hurtling towards Earth and wanted me to build him an atomic rocket ship to take people and animals to a new planet."

"Ha! That's crazy. What did you tell him?"

"I told Noah I was too busy building a mole machine to explore the world inside our hollow Earth."

Stockwell laughed, and it brought a smile to the face of the frustrated Williams. "Some people will believe anything, huh?"

Williams joined in the laughter. "They sure will."

Stockwell shook his head. "Another planet, huh. But, seriously, how is the work on the mole machine going?"

"We've figured out the air scrubber. It should prevent suffocation while transitioning to the inner world. We still need to figure out the orientation instrumentation. But you told me I had several months."

"You do. I'm not here about the mole man project. I need something else, and I'm afraid I need it right away." Damian pulled a folded sheet of paper from his inner pocket and unfolded the diagram across the office desk.

The flowers were in the way and he picked up the vase to move them. Their bouquet was sweet and kicked him in the brain. The mix of sweet flowers and elements from the shop mingled into a memory that he couldn't quite recall. But it made him happy.

"What's with the flowers?" he asked, as he cleared them from the desk.

"Oh, Roman broke his damn hand again. I tell you, that guy never learns. He keeps shoving his hand into the machines to fix 'em and getting it caught."

"Maybe you should fire him."

"I can't do that. I wouldn't be able to find anyone else willing to stick their hand into the machines."

"A good point," Stockwell conceded, as he set the plans across the open desktop.

Williams wiped some more grease on his hands with the shop rag and leaned over the sketch. "Damn, Dam. Doesn't this seem like overkill?"

"Sometimes overkill is just the right amount of kill."

Williams nodded. "This shouldn't be too difficult. It looks

like you've got all the tricky bits worked out. This power supply is revolutionary. Does it work?"

"It does."

"I'll get the boys to work on this right away. It shouldn't take too long."

"Thank you, Cam."

"Is there anything else you need?"

Stockwell nodded. "I need my great-grandpa's knuckles."

Williams put the rag back in his pocket. "I'll get the keys."

The two men walked from the shop, took a small elevator to the third floor and stepped out into the library.

If the lounge was the home of daydreams and big schemes, the library was where the work was done. The men here pored over various scripts and maps. They gingerly turned the pages of centuries-old texts, looking beyond the page for any clue that could lead them on their next adventure.

Stockwell breathed deeply the vanilla and almond notes of the aging paper and smiled at the memories that arose. Reading was one of his greatest passions. He devoured several books a day when not engaged with an adventure or some scientific puzzle, and the Vagabond library was one of his favorite places in the world.

The club's bookshelves held the history of the world. Ancient texts, codices, scrolls and tablets were at the beck and call of the members. The private journals of former members were also kept here for posterity.

Between the expansive shelves, glass cases held prized objects donated by members. Relics and written works were curated by the head librarian, but any gadgets and gizmos were Williams's department.

The two men crossed the quiet room and stared into one of the cases. "I doubt the generator still works," Williams said as he unlocked the display. "Your great-great-grandpa was really ahead of his time, but it's nearly a century old."

"I don't need the generator. Just give me the rest of it."

Williams opened the case and pulled the device from its

setting. He handed the pieces to Damian as a porter approached holding a phone on a silver platter.

"A call for you, Mr. Williams."

"Pardon me, Dam." Williams picked up the phone and began to walk from the library. "This is Williams." He rolled his eyes and waved to Damian. "I don't want a seat on your stupid rocket, Mr. Herndon."

Damian laughed and made his way to the back of the library where they kept a comprehensive periodical section. It was of little interest to those in search of fortunes, but to those hunting evil, the resource was invaluable.

The librarian saw him coming from across the room and the elderly clerk met him halfway to the reference desk. "Good evening, Mr. Stockwell. I've pulled the information you requested. It's over here."

"Thank you, Madison."

"I've also prepared a summary of the material. I hope that you'll find it helpful."

"I'm sure I will. As always."

Stockwell, a voracious reader, was nothing compared to Madison. The old man didn't read books. He absorbed them. Damian wondered if he ever bothered to open the covers or just gleaned their contents as he pulled them from the files.

His summaries were always spot on, even when Stockwell withheld the purpose of his research. He hated keeping secrets, but in the course of his work it was often necessary to withhold information to protect others. Many innocent people had died through the years for knowing too much, and Damian did all he could to never involve anyone in danger unless it was absolutely necessary for the greater good. Yet, somehow the librarian was able to see through the stories to the true puzzle.

He saw Stockwell to a table covered with leather-bound periodicals and pulled out a chair.

Damian sat. "Thank you, Madison."

"My pleasure, sir." He turned to leave but stopped and

offered his thoughts. "She seems like a wonderful woman, Mr. Stockwell."

Damian smiled. Once again the clerk had deduced the reason without even the smallest hint.

Madison returned to his desk, and Stockwell looked at the pile of material in front of him. He sighed at the volume before picking up the summary.

Madison had prepared a brief bio of Angelica Palmer. Her family had money and social status. But she had used it to pursue an education instead of a position of her own or invitations to social gatherings.

Seemingly antisocial, there was little written directly about her. Madison had instead made several deductions after looking at her body of work.

She had a bent for injustice—both legal and moral—that Stockwell could appreciate. She had tackled corruption in government and seemed to have a particular interest when politics and business crossed paths.

She was no fan of big business and seemed upset that trust-busting was no longer the national pastime it used to be. Angelica had made it no secret that her interest in his story was part of this crusade, and she seemed surprised when he granted her access. Damian knew he had nothing to hide and welcomed her perspective. The secrecy surrounding the project had only been a matter of timing. He was never trying to get away with anything more than a big launch for his new product.

The summary went on and highlighted several of her articles that Madison thought displayed her character in the clearest light. Damian began with those but left nothing at the table unread.

By early evening, he knew how she thought. He knew how she cared. Ultimately he believed her to be a champion of the defenseless, if a little misguided in identifying their enemy. But there was nothing to suggest that she would be party to a devious plot to supplant him with a robot doppelganger.

Something like that would be clear, if it were true. He began to doubt his own theory but dismissed this second-guessing, as he knew there was no one else who could have provided the information necessary to make the machine so stunningly accurate.

He pushed away from the table and thanked Madison for the help before realizing he was one of the last people in the library.

A quick glance at his wristwatch told him that the movement had run down. He shook it, then made a mental note to speak with the boys in engineering at DamTime to work on extending the line's power reserve.

Fortunately, Stockwell had trained himself to discern the time by the position of the sun. He had trained himself so well that he could even do it at night.

He stepped into the atrium and looked up through the massive skylight several stories above.

A rip of thunder echoed through the club. The sky had been holding its breath all day like a spoiled child, and it sounded as if the tantrum had finally arrived. The skylight above the atrium had grown dark, but the rain had not yet started.

It was late. It was about to be wet, and it was time to find Ms. Palmer and ask the journalist some questions of his own.

13

Blackmail, She Cried

Damian Stockwell believed that playing hard to get was a stupid game. Some people believed that the delayed gratification intensified the payoff. But the effort wasted was inevitably time regretted. And for someone like Damian Stockwell, who lived the majority of his life constantly facing death, it seemed strange to act uninterested just to build the tension.

It made him happy to see that Angelica Palmer felt the same way. She stood outside the Vagabond Club beneath an umbrella as the rain began to fall.

Damian didn't believe in umbrellas and let the rain fall on his face. He said nothing to the woman as the fresh rain stirred an earthy scent from the ground. Her appearance stirred other things.

He wanted to be angry. He knew he should be angry. He knew that he was angry with her and deep within him that anger burned. But he could not find a way to let it out like a gentleman.

There was no shortage of words to be had. He had never been more insulted. His look, his voice, his very self had been stolen by nefarious parties, and she had helped make it happen. He had been violated in the most personal of ways and only a few of them had been delightful. She deserved every harsh word he could hash out, but as he looked at her beneath the shimmer of the evening storm, he couldn't think of a word to say.

She spoke first. She had to yell over the thunder and rain. Her words were swallowed by the storm and she was forced to shout louder. "I think I have some explaining to do."

He crossed the sidewalk and stood in front of her. Despite the umbrella, the rain found its way onto her face. It ran down her cheek and found no imperfection in her skin. It was perfect. She was perfect.

Too perfect, perhaps? He needed to be sure.

Stockwell raised his hand. The test was the only way to be sure.

She turned to offer her cheek. She made no apologies and no pleas. She closed her eyes and waited for the slap.

He couldn't do it. She was a woman, after all, and only a coward struck a woman. He was no coward, and while there were always exceptions to a rule, there was rarely a good reason to strike a woman.

In the course of his life he had found only three.

The first was if the woman was a vampire or pretending to be a vampire, and through some confusion, deception or acquiescence to begging, had gotten too close to one's neck. In these cases a strike was acceptable, though technically it didn't really count as hitting a woman at all, as the undead were surprisingly gender neutral.

The second exception was if the woman in question had mental control of no less than three tigers—or similar large predatory cats—and was using said mind control powers to threaten others with immediate death. In this case, a sharp slap was the bare minimum required to break the mind control link and was acceptable in the name of the greater good. Admittedly, this one didn't come up often.

The third and final exception was a slap used in greeting or departure. This, of course, was not a welcome custom everywhere, but it was to a single, remote tribe in the Congo. The tribe consisted of a single woman named Grumlata who lived among the Virunga gorillas.

Now that Stockwell thought about it, it may have been less a tribal custom and more that Grumlata was a weirdo her tribe had sent to live in the jungle on her own because she kept slapping people all the damn time.

He desperately wanted to add a fourth exception to the rule, which stated it was okay to slap a woman to ensure that she was not a homicidal robot. But he knew how people were, and this exception would eventually be abused. He could picture cowardly men walking around, slapping unsuspecting women and then, with a shrug of their shoulders, saying, "I thought she was a robot." The bastards.

Damian could not be responsible for setting such a dangerous precedent. He lowered his hand.

Angelica, surely wondering why the slap had not come, looked back up. Her eyes were convincing. They were filled with regret and there seemed to be a smoldering pity buried deep inside that she wanted him to see. There was too much emotion for her to be anything but human.

"Thank you," she said. "I know I deserve it. For what I put you through. For how I—" She looked away, unable to finish the apology.

Stockwell helped. "For how you betrayed my trust? For how you made a mockery of my confidence? For how you manipulated me? For how you made me feel? For how you used me to further the agenda of a suspected madman with the ability to create lifelike replicas of humans and who, probably, will use those skills to further his own nefarious needs rather than employ them for the benefit of mankind with some sort of living history display or something?"

"Yes," she said. "All of that. I—"

Stockwell held up a finger. "I'm not done. For how you seduced me? For how you made me look and feel like an idiot? For how you took my trust and threw it on the floor, kicked it around for a little bit, and then stepped on it like nothing more than a butt to be extinguished? For stealing my very essence? My soul? And my heart?"

"I'm not proud of any of that. But I wanted you to know that I had a really, really good reason."

Maybe one slap, he thought. Just to be sure. No one would really blame him if he could explain it well enough.

"Can we go somewhere to talk?" she asked.

"Here is somewhere."

She leaned closer. "Somewhere a little more private."

Her moves weren't seductive. She didn't reach out to touch him or play with her hair. It wasn't a game this time. She was being as honest as she knew how to be.

"I don't see why you can't just lie to me here."

"It's not safe here," she said.

A crash of lightning lit up the sky and the thunder barked. The bolt was close. It had surely struck somewhere on the island.

"I've never felt safer," Stockwell said.

"Please, Dam. I'm in terrible danger. You've got to help me."

"Why?"

"Because that's what you do. That's who you are. You said so yourself. You fight for those that can't fight for themselves. You said that the only thing evil needs to succeed in this world is for you to do nothing. Are you really going to do nothing now?"

He smiled. He had said that. He'd said it often. It was his creed. And his words always sounded good when they came from someone else.

"What's so amusing?" she asked.

"You. You betrayed my confidence to help create a robotic

doppelganger—an evil robotic doppelganger, no less—and now you're begging for my help as if it never happened?"

She stepped closer. A wisp of her perfume dodged the raindrops and reached his nose. It was as sweet as he remembered. Rose petals and a rustic scent he couldn't quite place. It caught him off guard and he closed his eyes for perhaps a moment too long. When he opened them, she had moved closer. He was under the umbrella with her now. Their world had shrunk to a rainless circle merely a few feet in diameter.

"Please, Dam."

"How can I trust you now? What's changed?"

"People are trying to kill me."

"So?"

"So? That proves I'm telling the truth this time."

"No, it doesn't. People try to kill me all the time."

"Of course it does!"

"No, it just proves you've pissed off someone else! And as angry as I've been with you, I don't find that too hard to believe."

"Only bad people want to kill people, Dam."

"Or good people with a good cause."

She said nothing for a moment and then smiled and leaned in closer. "You don't want to kill me. Do you, Dam?"

That smell. Her skin.

"A little," he said.

"Do you really?"

"Of course n ... I want to strangle you, but I don't want you dead."

"Of course you do. That's what love is."

"You're a weird lady."

She looked down at her feet before peeking up from under her bangs. "So are you going to strangle me? Or are you going to help me?"

"Maybe both."

She smiled.

Damian looked away. "Dammit." He moved her aside and

opened the passenger door to his coupe. "Get in before I just go with the strangling thing."

She smiled and sat down. Damian waited for her to collapse the umbrella before closing the door and moving to the driver's seat. The engine roared to life, and he pulled into the dark, wet city streets.

"Thank you, Dam." She pulled off her hat and her hair fell perfectly into place. "I knew I could come to you."

"Enough about how wonderful I am. It's time to tell me what's going on. Who are you working for, and what do they want?"

"They want you," she said. "They want the great Damian Stockwell."

"I can't blame them, but what do they want with me?"

"They want to replace you."

"Why?"

"Because you're a powerful man."

"That is true."

"They want to control the world and they plan to do it by replacing the world's most powerful men and women with their own robotic versions. There's no telling who they've already replaced."

"Are you trying to tell me that these machines are already among us?"

"I'm afraid so."

"I guess I've thrown a wrench into their plans."

"I wouldn't be so sure. The machines aren't like anything I've seen. They're even more advanced than your Val-8. They're beyond anything anyone has been working on."

"I saw pieces of the Val-8 design in the me-bot. I'm assuming that the mysterious robotologists' deaths are a little less mysterious now. They've been taking the best designs and assimilating them into their own. The perfect pieces to make the perfect replicas."

"At this point there's no way to tell the machines from the

real men."

"Oh, there's a way." Damian stared at his hand and smiled before turning down an avenue. "And how are you mixed up in this, Miss Innocent?"

"It's my father."

"Your father is a robot?"

"Of course not. They've taken my father hostage." She turned away and looked out the window. "They told me if I ever wanted to see him again that I had to do what they said. I was supposed to learn everything I could about you. Every detail."

"Well, they certainly picked the right woman for the job."

"What would you have done if they took the person you loved most and threatened to kill them?"

"I'd have threatened to kill them right back. But I realize that's not an option for everyone."

"I'm sorry, Dam. But I'm not sorry I tried to save my father. No daughter could regret that." She turned away and looked out the window.

Damian dropped his head. He prided himself on having complete control of his body and everything in it. But he had let his emotions get the best of him. This woman had needed his help from the very beginning. Had he not been so blinded by his own bruised ego, he may have seen it sooner. He didn't know what to say. "I don't know what to say."

"I know I betrayed you, Damian. But now I'm asking for your help. And you're the only person that can help me."

"They wanted every detail?" he asked.

She looked back at him with a weak smile. "No. That was my idea."

"I'm prepared to help you. But how do I know you're not at it again? How do I know you're not just giving me this sob daddy kidnapping story to take more measurements?"

"When you stopped the machine in London, you set back their plans."

"What are their plans?"

"I don't know exactly. I've told you everything I was able to piece together."

"You seem to be pretty well informed for a victim. I've dealt with a lot of diabolical despots in my time and I'll tell you this, they don't usually gab about their plans to people they're blackmailing."

"Dam, I'm an investigative reporter. I've put as many of the pieces together as I could. This is what I do."

"Maybe," he nodded. "But I still don't trust you."

"They're trying to kill me!"

"You keep saying that, but we've been talking for some time and no one has tried to kill you yet."

Damian turned another corner. That's when the truck plowed into them.

14

Threat of Innocence

The truck speared the side of the Duesenberg and sent it rolling down the street. With each inversion, Damian was thankful he had chosen the coupe this evening and not his convertible. The steel roof held well enough as the chassis rolled over and over.

It crumpled and crushed and screamed, but it held.

Stockwell bounced around the cabin, feeling every jar and crash as it shrank around him. Even in this chaos he tried to help Angelica. Reaching out, exposing his arms and hands to further injury, he grabbed for the girl as she tumbled. The intelligent thing to do would be to pull his arms in close and ride out the momentum, but the intelligent thing and right thing, as they often are, were at odds.

Wrenching metal, squealing tires and breaking glass drowned out her screams. He heard nothing from her, the cries of fear, the groans or the utterances of pain, that she was surely making as the wreck went on.

His own wounds commanded him to shout out, but he gritted his teeth as the car beat him across his entire body and refused to give the pain and fear the satisfaction they felt they deserved.

The car slid to a stop against a lamppost. The passenger side was beneath them, and he looked through the shattered windshield for the truck that caused the accident. He couldn't see anything but an empty, rain-soaked street. The vehicle must be on the other side.

As the sounds of the wreckage faded, there came the eerie silence that followed a disaster and preceded accusations. In a few moments the air would be filled with blame, shouting and swearing, but for the moment, everyone involved was still processing what had happened. Stockwell defined tragedy as the moment when time and reality are ripped suddenly and violently apart. At that moment the two refuse to acknowledge one another like bitter, former lovers passing on opposite sides of the street, each with a new flame on their arm. The event is impossible to deny, but neither would ever admit its importance. There was always silence as those who witnessed the event waited for the two to come back together.

"Angelica!" She should be right below him, but he could not find her in the mangled interior. The seats had twisted and he had come to rest on the passenger seat frame. He grabbed desperately below him, trying to find her with his fingers.

Light and sound came rushing back through the silence as tragedy became reality. He could sense a fire. The licking of heat and the flutter of light mingled with the smell of spilt fuel and oil. He couldn't tell if it was his car or the truck that was now aflame, but he knew it didn't matter. If either exploded, the damage would affect them all.

"Angelica?" He reached beyond the twisted seat. "Answer me!"

There was a heavy thunk on the door above him. Whatever made the sound had also shifted the weight of the car, and he felt himself falling farther into the car as the wreckage squeaked around him. He reached out to stop the fall, fearing he would land on the girl. He caught the dashboard and turned around.

The driver's door screamed. The metal wasn't torn or twisted off—it was sheared away as if it had been cut with a torch. The man who'd done the shearing stood above the wreckage and tossed the door into the night, as if it weighed nothing. His suit was tattered and torn from the accident, but he moved without injury and pulled Stockwell from the car as if he weighed even less than the door.

The man was more than human and clutched Damian by the throat with a single hand. It lifted him out and held him over the car. Damian's feet dangled inside the cabin, trying to find a foothold.

The man's eyes were dead. They had no sparkle and sat in his face like an afterthought. His dark hair lay flat against his head with no bounce and no body. Everything else about the man was what Damian could only call simple. It was a face that could not be described, for it lacked any prominent feature. It was a dumb face.

Stockwell grabbed onto the wrist and tried to pull himself free. He tore at the arm's flesh and stripped it away, revealing a metal skeleton beneath.

The machine felt nothing. "You cannot stop us. We are stronger than you. We do not feel pain. We do not feel anything. We are better than you."

Behind the machine, the truck burned. Against the dance of the flames he could see movement. The truck was more of a twisted hulk than the car, and as Damian watched, the bent metal panels began to unfold.

Two more robots stepped from the wreck and moved toward the car. They had the same dumb face as the machine before him.

The machine's hand began to squeeze slowly around his throat. It could snap his neck in a fraction of a second but it was taking its time. What was this? Machines knew only efficiency. Masochism was a uniquely human vice. Something, someone had to be behind it. But who?

It didn't matter now. Quick or slow, the machine was going to kill him.

Damian's arms were bloodied and bruised. They felt separate from his body, but they still moved as he commanded. He welcomed the numbness because what he was about to do was going to hurt—if it didn't kill him altogether.

The leads for his great-grandfather's knuckles ran down the inside of his arms to a battery pack around his waist. A quick glance assured him they were still there, despite the tumble of the wreck.

Damian supported himself with one hand, then laid his forearm across the robot's wrist and took what breath he could. If it didn't work, he would never know.

He let go and slapped the switch at his waist. The battery pack sent a charge through the leads and into the machine's servos. They could have seized in their current position. They could have contracted with the voltage. But his desperate play had worked. The current ran through the machine and shorted out the arm, releasing its grip around his throat.

Stockwell fell against the roof of the car and rolled backward into the street. He scrambled to his feet and dug into his pockets as the two other machines leapt onto the wreck, shifting its weight once more.

Damian peered in through the busted windshield as he backed away, looking for any sign that Angelica was all right.

The first machine dropped to the ground. Its dead arm flopped at its side. "You cannot defeat us. Your tricks will not work on all of us."

"I haven't got any more tricks up my sleeve." Stockwell pulled his hands from his pockets and quickly attached the brass knuckles to the leads on his arms. "I'm just going to punch your stupid robot faces off."

The machine charged. Its still functioning arm reached for Stockwell's face.

Damian sidestepped the grab and threw a left cross into the

cheek of the machine. There was a satisfying clang as metal met metal and a shower of sparks exploded from the knuckles. The current burned through the robot's synthetic skin and exposed the brushed metal skull beneath.

The machine backed away and reached for its face.

"God, that felt good," Damian said.

The machine came for him again. A closed fist swung at Stockwell's head.

Ever the defiant victim, Damian bobbed and weaved around the blows and landed several jabs in the robot's face. Each strike exposed more and more metal until the human appearance was all but stripped away.

He could hear its mechanics whirring about as it tried to process the situation and find the best way to counter. It appeared to have come to a conclusion and punched again.

Stockwell ducked low and came up with a devastating upper cut that would change a man's diet and dental records. It was just enough to snap the robot's head back and send a final surge of electricity into the system.

The machine slumped forward and said nothing else.

Damian felt the belt around his waist warming up. He had taken the design from the black box's power supply and applied it to his belt. It should provide more than enough power to defend against the other two machines, but he had no idea how hot it would get.

The robotic duo watched the first machine fall to the ground and took a moment before dropping to the ground to press the attack.

Stockwell knew they were learning. The next generation of machines would be built to counter his attacks. The joints were too exposed to an electrical charge. The faces would most likely be hardened, and sensitive systems would be pulled further into the casings. Any machine he fought after tonight would be ready for his electrified fists. He would have to enjoy it while he could.

He smiled as they came at him together. The machines were

identical in height and build. Even their faces did little to set them apart. They attacked in perfect sync.

What few blows they managed to land hit harder than the Manassa Mauler, but the ringing sound their skulls made when he connected made the pain worthwhile.

Their fighting skills were sloppy. All fury and no style. Damian had a variety of styles to choose from. He had studied all over the world and could employ any number of techniques. But tonight, he just wanted to box. It had been years since he had stepped into a ring, but he soon found the familiar rhythm in the footwork and, even though his opponents made it easy, he found the exercise more than enjoyable.

His jabs cut the synthetic skin across their faces, and he delivered precision blows to their bodies and limbs. He felt the belt around his waist grow uncomfortably warm, but he fought on. Every hit caused a spark and the shutdown of some system within the machine.

Sometimes the system failure was obvious—a limb would lose control or stop working altogether. Other times the effect was something deeper—the machine would lean left or start turning in a circle. He enjoyed every malfunction he inflicted, but time was running out. He had to save the girl.

The final two blows were a guilty pleasure he would treasure for years. A right hook caught one machine behind the ear and its head exploded in an eruption of blue, white and red so brilliant that it brought the Star Spangled Banner to the front of his mind.

The second machine backed away, put its head down and charged.

Damian rolled to the side and struck it in the back of the knee as it passed.

The robot collapsed to the ground and slid into the curb before exploding in a rush of flames.

Stockwell deactivated the knuckles and pulled the belt from around his waist as he rushed back to the car. He reached the overturned Duesy just as the other two machine men began to burn.

"Self destruct?" he muttered. "Another new trick." He turned his attention back to the woman. He had not heard her screaming or calling out for help. The roof was crushed to the hood of the car and he couldn't see anything through the windshield.

Shouting for her, he climbed back to the top of the driver's side door. "Angelica! Angelica! It's going to be okay. I'm here. I'm here and I believe you. They really were trying to kill you."

He reached the opening and leaned into the car. A lock of red hair was visible beneath the passenger seat. It wasn't moving.

Damian worked his way back into the cabin. "It's going to be okay, Angelica!"

Flexing his mighty arms, he pulled against the steel frame of the seat. It groaned in protest as he bent it back and exposed the motionless body of Angelica Palmer.

He closed eyes and shook his head. "Dammit."

15

An Interesting Interrogation

Bertrand opened the door, panting as if he had just raced across the expansive home in some petty and desperate attempt to beat The Bertron to the chore. The Bertron stood close behind him, still reaching for the knob.

Stockwell stood before the valets soaked with rain and covered in grime. His clothes were tattered, bloody rags hanging from his frame and cut in a thousand places. His bruised and beaten state was nothing compared to the look he wore on his face. A canvas bag was slung over his shoulder.

"Sacre bleu. What 'appened?"

"I found the girl." Damian pushed his way past Bertrand and handed the canvas bag to The Bertron. "Take it to my lab."

The machine bore the weight of the bag without a sound and went upstairs.

"She did zis to you?" Bertrand asked. "What did you zay to

'er?"

"She didn't do this to me. A truck did this to me. And I was assaulted by three more of those diabolical machines tonight." He gestured for his friend to follow him up the stairs. "They're either getting smarter or they're becoming less stupid. I can't tell which."

"'ow did you stop zem?"

"Great-Great-Grandpa's knuckles," Stockwell chuckled. "That old man sure knew what he was doing."

"Zey worked?"

"Spectacularly. With a little help from some modern know how. You should have seen it, Bertrand. It was like the Fourth of July. But instead of being some gawking spectator in the crowd, I was up in the sky. I was the explosive force declaring freedom for all. Every punch was an exhibition. It was majestic."

They reached the top of the stairs and the Frenchman smiled. "You got your fist back."

Stockwell held the lab door open as his dour expression was replaced by a crooked smile. "I got my fists back."

Bertrand stepped into the lab with Damian. "What about ze girl?"

"Oh." Stockwell pointed to the canvas sack as The Bertron set it on the workbench. "She's in the bag."

"What?" Bertrand rushed over to the workbench. "She eez dead?"

"No," Stockwell stood next to him and found the zipper. "But I couldn't save her legs." He opened the bag and rolled the contents onto the workbench.

Angelica Palmer's torso landed face down on the metal surface with a distinct clank.

Bertrand shrieked at the horror he anticipated before realizing that the woman was yet another machine.

"Bertrand, please compose yourself." Damian sat the limbless torso upright on the bench.

"I apologize, Monsieur. I waz expecting … she eez a robot?"

Stockwell slapped the Angelicabot across the face. "Yep."

"You can't stop us, Stockwell. It's too late. We are everywhere." The machine let out a maniacal laugh. There was a loud click from somewhere inside the torso. Then nothing happened.

"What waz zat?" the valet asked.

"She was trying to activate her self-destruct mechanism." He held a small capsule the size of a baby carrot and smiled. "But she doesn't realize that I removed it during her temporary deactivation. I'm not an idiot, my dear Angelica."

Damian tossed the capsule in the trash, where it shattered and burst into flames. Stockwell blew on the fire twice, to no affect.

"The Bertron," he called.

The machine stepped back into the lab and awaited instructions.

Stockwell slid the flaming trash can across the room with a gentle kick. "Take care of that, will you?"

The Bertron complied and set to extinguishing the flames as Damian turned back to the workbench. A pensive look appeared on his face. "What was I saying?"

"How you're not an idiot," Angelica's head said. "Then you set your own lab on fire."

"That's enough out of you." Damian picked up a shop rag from the bench and shoved it in her mouth.

"I can't believe she eez une robot."

"Actually, looking back now, it's obvious. She was often cold and distant during our interviews. She was almost too methodical in her methods. She never once complained about being cold. And her lovemaking was very rhythmic and pinchy."

"You 'ad no zuzpicions?"

"Well, she was awfully heavy. But it's rude to mention a woman's weight, Bertrand. You're French. I thought you had manners."

Bertrand sighed. "Pardon. I forget myzelf."

"That's better. Besides, if I had mentioned it she would have stopped what she was doing."

The torso on the workbench grunted.

"You just zaid eet waz not good."

"True. But a bad day golfing … right?" Stockwell elbowed the Frenchman in the rib.

"You are not worried?"

Stockwell turned to look at him. "Why should I be worried?"

Bertrand shrugged.

"Oh, my God!" Stockwell snapped. "What if I got gremlins?"

"I don't zink zat eez 'ow gremlins work."

"Are you sure?"

"Very sure."

"Well, you're French. You would know."

"What does zat …? I will not stand 'ere and—"

"Still," Stockwell said. "Better safe than sorry." He turned to the machine by the smoldering trash can. "The Bertron. Call the doctor and set an appointment as soon as possible. An ounce of prevention and all that."

"Monsieur," Bertrand said. "Perhaps you are overreacting?"

Stockwell ignored his trusted friend and employee and turned back to the robot on his workbench. "Do you have, or do any of your robosexual partners have, or ever had, gremlins?"

The Angelica answered but the rag muffled her response.

Stockwell ripped it from her mouth and pointed a finger at her. "Repeat that. Now."

"I said, go to hell."

Stockwell shoved the rag back in her mouth before turning to Bertrand. "Damn robots."

"'ow did you dizcover she waz a robot?" he asked.

Stockwell smiled. "My friend, when you know women as well as I do, it becomes a simple matter of observation. When I swooped in to save her from the car, I could easily tell."

"Ahh, Monsieur, I know what you're zaying. You can zee eet een 'er eyes, when she looks zat you. Ze windows to zee soul could nevair be duplicated. Not such a work of ze almighty. And een 'er voice you can tell. Ze quavers, ze pleading notes buried, but not buried, zat zay, 'Take me. My soul eez yours. Be gentle, for eet eez fragile, but be firm, because soft eez not zo good.'"

Damian nodded. "Yes. That's exactly what I meant."

"Oui. Eet eez always like zis."

"That, and I ripped her robot arms off when I tried to pull her out of the wreckage."

"Oh, no."

"No, really. Tore 'em right the hell off."

"Mon Dieu!"

"Scared the hell out of me at first. I even considered benching less for a moment. But then I was like, 'oh she's a robot,' and here we are."

"So, what eez next?"

"Next we find robot city and destroy this mechanical menace once and for all, before they replace the world's leaders with their detestable duplicates that could very well pave the way for a takeover of all mankind."

"Oui. Zis we should do. Where did she zay eet waz?"

"She didn't." Stockwell turned up his palms and dropped them to his knees. "She's been woefully unhelpful ever since I ripped her arms off."

Angelica's head mumbled an insult that was clear despite the mouthful of rag.

Damian pointed to her. "You see? That's exactly the attitude I'm talking about."

"Oui. Eet eez 'orrible."

Damian clapped his hands before saying, "But the truth is, we don't need her to tell us anything, as I have already deduced the city's location on my own."

"'ow?" Bertrand asked.

"Smell her," Stockwell said.

"Pardon, Monsieur?"

"Smell her," he repeated.

Bertrand leaned in before stepping away. "I don't want to smell 'er."

"Go on. Give her a sniff."

Bertrand was hesitant. Even if she was a robot, the action seemed a little forward. But Stockwell kept gesturing, so he leaned in close and took a quick sniff as the robot grumbled. He shook his head. "I'm only getting ztinky rag."

"Oh." Stockwell pulled the rag out of Angelica's mouth, unleashing a slew of horrible words and insults. "There you go. Get that nose in there."

"You are such a pig," Angelica spat.

"Ignore her, Bertrand."

Bertrand leaned in again and sniffed cautiously, fearing lingering rag. There was a scent that raised his eyebrows and he sniffed deeper. It was sweet and exotic, while at the same time musky and familiar.

"Are you about done, Pierre?" asked Angelica.

Bertrand stood up. "Eet's ... eet's intoxicating."

"Isn't it? A bouquet of sweet flowers mixed with the smell of invention and cowboys."

"Oui. Zat eez exactly eet. What eez zat? And why doez it taunt me zo?"

"It's a mixture of perfume, gear oil and leather. And it taunts you because you're a man." Stockwell picked up a utility knife from the workbench. "Watch." He held the knife to the robot's face.

Angelica cried, "What are you doing?"

"Calm down, I'm just going to cut off some of your face."

"You do and I'll kill you!"

"What are you going to do? You don't have any arms." He pushed the blade into her cheek.

She screamed.

Stockwell pulled back the knife. "Oh, please. That doesn't hurt. You've never felt anything, not a day in your life."

Angelica looked away. "Well, that hurt."

Damian put the knife back in her cheek and cut away a square section of skin. He held it out to Bertrand.

The valet turned it over in his hands. It was smooth and blemish free on the outside and rough on the inside.

"See?" Stockwell asked. "It's nothing more than leather. The tanning process is obviously something new, but it's just good old boot leather."

Bertrand felt the skin and sniffed it. "Oui. Eet eez leather."

"And here," Stockwell pointed to the exposed inner cheek. "You can see here how all the gears need constant lubrication. Otherwise her lies would stop."

"Oh, get over it. Like I'm the first woman to ever lie to you." Oil leaked from the cheek and ran down Angelica's face as she spoke.

"And ze sweet scent?"

"Good old-fashioned perfume." Stockwell pulled back the robot's red hair and pointed to a small nozzle behind the ear. "I have no doubt there's an internal atomizer designed to mask the smell of robot. But it failed to cover the construction completely and unintentionally drove me wild."

"We meant to do that," Angelica said.

"Yeah, right," Damian said.

"We did!"

"Did you mean to lose your arms too, you lying hussy?"

Angelica began to sob.

"Monsieur, zat eez not nize."

"Don't you take her side on this, Bertrand. She betrayed me. She used me. And in only a somewhat satisfying way." Stockwell's memory drifted away to a smile for a moment but it quickly turned sour. "But now it's my turn to use her body against her and her kind."

"I don't zink I want to watch zat."

"Don't be so immature, Bertrand. With these clues at my disposal, I can tell you exactly where we need to go next."

"Where? Where could zuch inhumanity exist?"

"France."

Bertrand slapped the flap of skin down on the desk and backed away. "I am tired of your inzults about my ..."

"Grasse, France, to be specific," Stockwell continued. "The perfume capital of the world. They produce two-thirds of your nation's natural aromas. Its micro-climate is perfectly suited for growing the necessary flowers. Do you know of it?"

"Oui. Of courze I know of eet."

"Oh, then you must know why they became the perfume capital of the world. And you must know why they started growing so many flowers."

Bertrand stumbled over several answers before committing to a sullen, "Non."

"Because it stinks," Stockwell said. "Smells god-awful."

"Still wiz ze inzults?"

"Not at all. The town's first industry was leather tanning. Dead animals smell, my friend. It doesn't matter what country they're from. So Grasse grew flowers. Fields and fields of them, to cover up the stench of their labor. Then they used it to scent the leather itself." Stockwell shrugged. "The perfume industry developed from there."

The clues aligned in Bertrand's mind and he grew excited. "So zey have aczez to zenturies of tanning exzperience—enough to pozzibly create zomething like zis." He picked up the skin flap. "And zey have ze perfume knowledge to create an intozicating mask for ze zmell."

"Well done, Bertrand. I am impressed."

Bertrand smiled and felt a touch of pride. "Thank you, Monsieur."

"Of course, I just recreated the perfume, analyzed and traced the manufacturer. But your way works, too. Just not as fast as mine. And we don't have much time to waste. We're going to France. I'll need you to pack our things."

Bertrand stood a little taller. "Not Ze Bertron?"

"Please, my friend. We are packing to confront an evil force that controls an army of robots in the south of France. I can't entrust this to him."

Bertrand straightened up and beamed. "I appreciate zat, Monsieur."

"The Bertron has no fashion sense, and this is France we're talking about, after all."

Bertrand shrunk. "Oui. Are we done 'ere?"

"Almost. There's just one last matter." Stockwell turned to the torso of Angelica Palmer. "Apologize."

"What?" she asked.

"You heard me. You betrayed my trust. You played with my emotions. Now apologize."

She spoke clear and slow. "No."

"Now!" Stockwell slammed his feet into the workbench, causing a tremendous rattle.

"I'll rust first."

"I don't zink we have time for zis, Monsieur."

Damian sighed. "Fine." He picked the body up from the workbench and carried it across the room.

"What are you doing? Where are you taking me?"

"Bertrand is right. We don't have time for this." He set her down on a chair. "But I expect an apology when I get back. So practice."

"Practice? What the hell are you talking about?"

He rotated her body to face the remains of the Stockwellbot from London. "Just look me in the eyes and practice."

"No. Turn me the other way." A quick series of clicks fired within her as she tried to activate her missing self-destruct capsule.

"Practice," Stockwell said one final time and left the room over her cursing and idle armless threats.

16

Smells Like Grasse

The Cote d'Azure: holiday destination and playground of the rich. If it were a rung on the social ladder, it would be just below the one labeled "Not a Step." It was a dream for many that would only be experienced in the gossip rags. And even if those dreamers were to travel to this sun-kissed stretch of sand in Southern France, it would seem no more real than it was in their imaginations.

Royalty and the world's elite gathered on France's southern coast to test the adage that money couldn't buy happiness. They arrived by yacht and private railcar with suitcases full of fortune and did their best to spend it in an attempt to forget their worries for a short stretch of time. They dined and slept in opulence, they partied into the night with balls and galas, and, by the end of the trip, they had proved very little to anyone but appeared happy nonetheless.

On the advice of doctors, the rich came as a treatment for

any of a litany of illnesses from bronchitis to ennui, and as they indulged, they toasted to one another's health and praised their physicians for such a fine diagnosis.

"Ah, the Cote d'Azure," Stockwell mused. "One of my favorite destinations. Many Americans think it means French Riviera, you know."

"Eet doez not," said Bertrand.

"But it doesn't. It means azure coast. I'll bet you didn't know that."

"Of courze I knew zat. I just zaid—"

"Learn something new every day." Damian smiled. "That's my philosophy."

The plane's hull cut into the impossibly blue waters of the Mediterranean. Ribbons of white trailed behind the Clipper in the calm waters as the flying boat made its way to the dock.

Stockwell peered out the window at the city of Cannes. Once quaint, its popularity among the world's most notable was seen in the development along its shore, if one could see the development past the ever-present flotilla of magnificent yachts at anchor in the harbor.

Private villas dotted the hillside in greater numbers than he had previously seen. Hotels occupied the beachfront, and their properties spread out, offering most guests a view of the sea.

Damian sighed. He'd spent many a fine night on this coast. And each and every one had produced a tale worthy of a memoir.

He had dined with royalty and shared many a tale with barons and earls, lords and ladies. One time he went fishing with a viscount, and by the end of the trip they had become close friends. Though he still had no idea what a viscount was.

While the idea of a monarchy angered the American in him and made his red-blooded hackles stand up, he found the people polite, congenial and generous, with very few exceptions. Particularly baronets. They seemed to always have a chip on their shoulders.

He had gambled with Rothschildren, who were surprisingly

horrible gamblers. Having gambled with the fate of nations and the course of history itself, Damian was surprised to find the family so terribly bad at poker. You wouldn't think such a renowned dynasty would get so twitchy around a few thousand francs.

He had painted with Matisse and Picasso. The bright colors and clean light of the area had brought many artists to the coast, and Stockwell spent hours with brush in hand pioneering his own artistic movement: Damism. The men would laugh together and offer advice to one another. Picasso seemed focused on asking Damian if he had not put too many bullets or explosions in his piece, while Damian constantly tried to remind Pablo that noses went on the front of the face. Even now the memory made him laugh.

"What eez funny, Monsieur?"

"That Picasso," Stockwell said. "He never learned."

The Clipper pulled up to the dock and the pair disembarked. It was clear right away that news of the world's economic woes had not yet reached the city of Cannes.

A line of long dark limousines idled near the shore, awaiting their passengers with open trunks and drivers at the ready. Bertrand searched the line and offered a quizzical "Hmmm." He looked down the street and shrugged. "I will locate our driver, Monsieur."

"No need, Bertrand. Transportation has been arranged. We just need to wait for our luggage here."

The passengers stepped immediately from the plane to their cars, so accustomed to the climate that few bothered to take a deep breath and soak in their surroundings.

Those that weren't destined for private villas would soon be doted upon at the finest hotels. They would never touch their luggage. It would be sent up and unpacked by hotel or house staff. When it was time to leave, a servant would clean and pack it for them again.

The Clipper's crew unloaded the cargo hold as the line of cars thinned, leaving nothing but a canvas-covered truck rumbling in the line.

"That's us," said Damian. "Have them load the luggage in the back. I'll get the keys."

●●●

Grasse wasn't far from Cannes, but as the truck meandered through the hills of Southern France, it felt as if they were in a different world. They were only twenty miles from the coast but had already climbed a thousand feet, as the Alps began their seven-hundred-fifty-mile journey across the sky.

The valleys created a distinct climate from that of the coast, which made the city an ideal location for its horticultural endeavors. Even in the truck they could feel the sea air give way to something fresher and more fertile.

The humidity quickly made the cab unbearable, and the two men rolled down their windows. The smell of seven million flowers filled the air. In one quick sniff, Damian detected myrtle, lavender and jasmine. Then the wind shifted, and he smelled several colors of roses, orange blossom and wild mimosa.

He knew there were more, but he was not as trained in smelling as he had wished. It was a skill he had always planned to work on, and Grasse would be the perfect place for such training.

Here "Le Nez" were trained to distinguish over two thousand smells. Such training could prove invaluable to him in the future, and he made a mental note to return one day, when the danger wasn't so imminent.

He took a deeper breath and smiled. He loved the smell of nature and let the scents dance around his mouth and nose before exhaling with a mighty smile. "Just smell that, Bertrand. That's Mother Nature's perfume. And she's placed it all around us to cover the stench of humanity. I'd be offended if I didn't enjoy it so."

Bertrand nodded and dabbed at the corner of his eyes with a

handkerchief. His eyes were red and puffy, and his nose dripped with a regular rhythm.

"What's wrong with you?" asked Stockwell.

"I am allergic."

Stockwell laughed. "Baby."

The truck crested a hill and the full beauty of Grasse became visible. Fields of color filled the slopes and pastures around the town. Brilliant blues, reds, yellows, purples and more rose and fell with the hillsides. The town produced thousands of tons of flowers each year, and they used every bit of space to deliver on the demand.

"It's amazing. Look at that, Bertrand."

"My eyez are swollen, Monsieur."

"Baby."

They rolled into town and passed a sign welcoming them to La capital mondiale des parfums. It was quickly evident why it was deserving of the title. Signs for the Galinard, Molinard and Fragonard perfumeries were visible from the Route Napoleon. And below them, in the old town, were many other purveyors of fine odors. One of which hid a deeper secret than formulas for perfume.

Stockwell drove to the center of town and parked the truck. The narrow street dated back more than six hundred years and was now effectively blocked.

"Monsieur, you are blocking ze road."

"I don't know if you've noticed through your oh so delicate eyes, my friend, but we haven't seen another vehicle since entering the town." Stockwell opened the door and stepped onto the ancient street. "In fact, I haven't seen many people at all. Maybe they're all at work stomping on flower pedals."

"Eez zat how zey do eet?"

Damian shrugged and walked around to the back of the truck. Three stories above them, a shutter opened and an elderly woman leaned out from the window to cast her nosey eye upon them.

Stockwell waved with a smile. "Bonjour, Madame."

The woman said nothing and made no move to return the wave. She withdrew into the window and pulled the shutters closed behind her.

"Not very friendly, are they?" he asked Bertrand.

Bertrand nodded. "Zomezing doezn't feel right 'ere."

"That's to be expected. When an evil organization secretly moves into a town this size, the populace is often threatened into submission. It could be overt blackmail or the threat of violence. But even the overwhelming presence of evil will put a chill on the friendliest people. It's time to check out the perfumery and find out what stinks in Grasse."

The two men strolled down the tight and winding corridors of the town. Its location on the slope of the mountain made for steep streets, and pathways leading away from the main avenue were filled with stairs that had been built for people of a shorter age. Damian found himself tripping on the short steps before deciding to take them three at a time.

More people began to fill the streets as they went. The populous went about their business, moving in and out of the shops and markets, but there was something eerie about it all.

"Zey are zo quiet," Bertrand said. "Eet eez creepy."

"It is that." Stockwell leaned in close to Bertrand and whispered, "We don't know how much of the town has been infiltrated. Any of these people could be robots. Let me know if any of these people are acting unFrench."

"Zey are all acting strange."

"Obviously. But let me know if anything seems out of the ordinary."

The crowd paid little attention to the men as they passed through the town center. Stockwell had to admit it was a pleasant-smelling town. The aroma of flowers and oils wafted from the storied perfume shops, and a change in the breeze would delight with an entirely new combination.

"Where ezactly are we heading?" Bertrand asked.

"I'm sure you've noticed the stores we've been passing. This town is filled with perfume makers that have been around for years." Stockwell pointed out several shops in succession. "Molinard is nearly a hundred years old. Galinard, nearly two hundred years. And, aside from having the funniest name, Fragonard is a relative newcomer, but they've been in business for almost a decade."

"So?"

"So, when I first got wise to Angelica's scent, I traced the perfume back to its manufacturer, and I discovered that the manufacturer has been in business for less than a year. I've deduced that they are the source behind the evil we seek." Stockwell stopped and pointed to the shop in front of them. "And here we are."

"What waz your first clue?"

Damian studied the sign above the shop. Robonard, establish 1933. "Well, of course it seems obvious now. But, before it … it took some reasoning."

Bertrand's eyes were puffy and shiny. Any expression he wore was swallowed by his own face, but Stockwell could tell the valet was passing judgment. Damian cleared his throat. "Hindsight and all."

Bertrand may have blinked, he couldn't be sure.

"Shut up, Bertrand. Wait here. Two men walking into a perfume shop together might look as weird as your face does." Stockwell opened the door to the shop and stepped inside.

The scent, her scent, the angel's scent, hit him with a wave of memories. The aroma filled the shop and for a moment he let it take him back to a simpler time, when he didn't know that he was in a torrid relationship with a robot.

"Bonjour, Monsieur. Comment puis-je vous aider?" the man behind the counter asked. His voice was nothing special. Nothing familiar. But his face was impossible to forget.

The dead eyes. The dark, flat hair. The plain and simple face. He had seen it three times before in the same evening. It was the same dumb face the robots wore when they rammed his car.

"Sorry, no."

The transition from French to English was seamless. In one breath, the man behind the counter lost all trace of an accent and spoke in a completely different voice. "Can I show you something?"

"I'm sorry. It seems my nose has led me astray." Stockwell turned back toward the door. He bumped into another Robonard salesman.

He had the same dead eyes. Same dumb face. And the exact same voice. "Are you certain, sir?"

"I'm afraid I just don't smell what I'm looking for here." Damian opened the door, stepped into the street and looked at the people milling about the town.

A grocer across the street had a similar lack of features as the men in the shop. So did a man strolling towards him.

He looked at the women and quickly noticed similarities in their appearance. Some of the other men looked different than the sales staff but similar to one another.

All told, he counted only eight distinct faces in a growing crowd of dozens.

Bertrand stepped up beside him. "What did you find, Monsieur?"

"Trouble, my friend," he said calmly. "We should probably head back to the truck."

The grocer across the way stood up from behind his cart and began to walk toward them. The Robonard shop doors opened behind them and the two employees stepped into the street.

"And we should probably run."

17

Smell of Evil

It was like running through a field of flowers, if the flowers in question were trying to kill you. Though in peril, Stockwell still found the aroma of the town delightful.

The entire population had turned on them. The crowd outside the perfume shop had stood and lurched toward the interlopers. The sight of several dozen similar faces staring at them had been unnerving, and when the crowd reached out with mechanical arms, the two men had run.

Their pursuers said nothing as they chased the pair through the narrow streets of the ancient city, but the rhythmic sound of their feet bashing against the cobblestones drove the two men on.

Damian finally risked a glance over his shoulder and saw dust rising behind each machine as they ground the ancient stones to powder. He slowed his step and turned.

The machines were pursuing, all of them—the grocer, the

strollers, the perfume shopkeepers—but they weren't running. They trod forward in sync, causing a terrifying beat that made the buildings shake, but it was obvious they were not built for speed.

"Bertrand," he called to his companion as they rounded a corner. "Slow down."

The valet slowed and the pair eventually stopped and turned. Damian pointed to the empty street behind them. "Look at this."

"I cannot zee anyzing," Bertrand said through puffy eyes.

"Exactly." Damian looked down the corridor. He could hear them coming and feel the march of their steps reverberating in the ground. But not one machine had rounded the corner. "Man, these things are pokey."

"You wish zey were fazter?"

"Of course not." Stockwell stared down the street and spoke to himself. "They must be older models."

The steady pounding of the mechanical mob beat on, but it was moments before they rounded the corner.

"It looks like we can take our time." Damian smiled. He stepped over to a storefront, put his hand on the door handle and joked, "Want to do some shopping?"

He pulled open the door and a little old lady tackled him to the ground. Her weight was tremendous and stank of perfume and motor oil.

"Do not resist. Do not resist." The mechanical voice droned on in the tone and timbre of a man half her age. Her small hands were trying to find a place around his neck. "Do not resist."

"Bertrand, get it off me! Get it off!"

Stockwell saw the valet's foot connect with the little old lady's head, and half of her face cracked away. The machine's workings churned on as she persisted in her warning, "Do not resist."

"Bertrand, how many of these things have you kicked in the face, and when has it ever worked?"

"Oui, Monsieur." Bertrand spun around. He may have been squinting, but it was hard to tell. He ran off down a side street and shouted, "Une moment."

"It wasn't a yes or no question!" Stockwell held back the little old lady's hands. She wasn't as strong as the Val-8, but her might could be equal to his own.

After a few moments of struggle it was clear that she was winning. The pruned hands inched closer to his neck and soon found their way around his throat.

He could feel the vibrations of the oncoming army through his back. Debris between the cobblestones began to bounce with every step they took. They would be on him soon, and if the little old lady didn't get him, the mob would.

"Do not resist," she said again.

Then came a rumble. Not from the approaching horde. It was a constant noise, and it was getting louder.

The little old lady squeezed, and he turned his head to try and find a breath. The rumble grew louder and he finally understood what it was.

The flower cart was careening down the side street, dropping petals and bouquets with every bump and jar of its wooden wheels. It was coming straight for them.

"Bertrand, you idiot!" His strength, intelligence and his good looks wouldn't be enough now. He had to count on luck. Luck that the wheels of the cart would cross around him and not over him. Luck that there would be enough clearance beneath the axle for one person but not for two. Luck that the little old lady wouldn't see it coming until the last second.

Stockwell pushed with all of his considerable might against the little old lady as the rumble grew into a roar.

"Do not—"

The cart rolled over them both and moved on, dragging the machine with it as it went. Damian found himself lying on the reverberating ground, looking up into a clear blue sky. Several rose petals fluttered down and came to rest on his chest and face. He took a deep breath and blew one from his lips as Bertrand ran to help him up.

"A flower cart?!"

"I could not find un Cadillac."

"What the hell were you thinking?" Damian yelled. "You weren't even steering."

"Eet worked, non?"

"Yes. But if it didn't, my obituary would say I was killed by a runaway florist wagon. A florist wagon! I'd never live that down."

"Eet worked," Bertrand repeated, and pointed to the wreckage of the cart.

The cart shifted. More flowers fell as it was shoved aside and the little old lady stood up.

A door crashed open behind them, and another older woman stepped into the street. Shutters above them slammed against the wall as a man scrambled out the window and fell to the street below.

The earth shook and the mob behind them rounded the corner, turning the ground beneath them to dust. The mob had grown.

"Maybe we should consider running again."

"Oui, Monsieur."

The two men ran as more machines poured into the streets from the surrounding shops and residences. They dropped from the upper windows onto the growing mob. The rumble became a tremble as more feet joined the march.

The machines began to appear ahead of them.

"Zey are everywhere!" Bertrand shouted as he ducked under the arms of a middle-aged robot.

"We'll be okay when we reach the truck." Stockwell rolled under the grabbing arms of a young woman wearing a blank expression. He sprang to his feet and kept running. "We're almost there."

The streets were all but full now. At least a hundred machines were behind them, and still more emerged as they raced through the town.

The truck had remained untouched and unguarded by the machines, and they ran for the covered bed.

Stockwell slammed against the gate and began to fumble with the locks.

Bertrand bounced on the balls of his feet as he watched. "What are you looking for?"

The gate dropped with a clang and Stockwell jumped in the back of the truck. "Won't be a minute. Watch out for the old woman."

"What?" Bertrand turned as a woman behind the second-story shutters dropped to the ground. He put up his arms as she grabbed for his throat. Seizing his wrists, the machine twisted and threw the valet up the street.

Damian grabbed a steel-colored case and drew it towards him. "Keep her distracted for me."

Bertrand landed on his back and slid across the cobblestones. The woman was coming toward him.

"What should I do?" he asked.

"Hit her with a flower wagon," Stockwell replied, as he snapped open the case's locks.

"Zat eez not helpful," Bertrand said as the robot punched for his head. He stepped aside and watched the woman's hand sink into the brick wall behind him.

"I know it isn't." He pulled the item out of the case and held it up. Williams had not let him down.

Bertrand rolled along the wall to dodge another blow and found himself in a corner.

The old woman drew back her fist.

He had nowhere to go.

The first report rolled through the streets, drowning out the stomp of the approaching horde.

The robot in front of him shook but did not stop. She struck.

The second round crackled through the air.

The old woman shuttered and froze. Her fist was a mere inch from Bertrand's face.

There was a third boom from the truck.

"You're going to want to move, Bertrand."

The valet ducked under the robot's arm as Stockwell cracked open a shotgun barrel. Three shells ejected from the breach and fell to his feet.

Bertrand jogged towards the truck. "What ze 'ell eez zat?"

"It's a triple-barreled shotgun." Damian pulled a red shell from a pouch at his side. "The first round is a gelatic acid. It eats away at their metal shell."

He jammed the red round into the left barrel and pulled a white one from the pouch. "The second round contains an electrical charge that will short out their system and render them completely, one hundred percent inoperative."

He slammed the white round into the right chamber and pulled a blue shell from the pouch. He slid it into a third barrel, centered beneath the first two.

"And what eez ze blue one?"

"High explosives."

"What eez zat for?"

He snapped the barrel shut. "Because I hate them, Bertrand."

The old woman exploded. Robot body parts flew around the narrow street. Her head rolled down the slight hill to Damian's feet.

He kicked her head away. "I really, really hate them."

The roar of the explosion faded quickly and the stomp of the approaching army grew louder. They would be upon them in seconds.

Stockwell dug back into the case and produced a second triple-barreled shotgun. He tossed it to the Frenchman and lobbed a pouch of shells after it. "Remember, it's red, white and blue. In that order. And as tempting as it is to shoot them in the face, it's better to aim for the chest."

Bertrand loaded the shells into the barrel and locked it into place.

"Now, put these down your pants." He handed Bertrand two

strips of metal. Each strip had a wire attached to the end.

"Monsieur?"

"Do it. Let the end drop to your feet and attach the straps to your laces. Run the wire to your waist."

Bertrand did as he was told, while Damian pulled a battery belt out of a bag in the truck. He attached the wires and fastened the belt around the valet's waist.

Stockwell placed three large boxes of the colored shells on the ground in front of the truck and jumped inside.

Bertrand knelt down within reach of the ammunition.

The mechanical mob rounded the corner. Their numbers had grown, and Bertrand was so stunned at the sight that he almost dropped his accent. "Zere are zo many."

18

Blaze of Grasse

A dozen faces looked at them from a hundred bodies. What could only be the entire population of Grasse marched toward them in lockstep, pounding their metal feet into the ancient stone of the avenue.

The street rumbled. The balconies rattled. The shutters shuddered. The red, white and blue shells bounced in the ammo boxes in front of the two friends.

The sweet scent of a million flowers was soon choked out by the dust the mechanical mob had stirred up. The dryness made Stockwell's eyes water but seemed to help override Bertrand's allergies.

"Remember to aim for the chest!" Damian shouted, then he pulled the first trigger.

The barrel blazed a pre-shaped gel of highly corrosive acid through the air. He fought the instinct to fire again; he had to wait for the first slug to do its work.

A young man in casual wear took the hit without flinching. His shirt began to smolder and char as the acid ate away at the metal beneath.

Damian fired again. And an electrical slug, built with technology ripped from the mysterious black box, sparked as it found its way into the newly formed hole.

The robot's body jiggled as the charge ran through its system, blowing tubes and rendering diodes inoperable. The machine stopped and the horde began to swarm around it.

Damian fired again and sent the explosive charge into the cavity.

The young manbot's place in the mob was perfect. Heartless, the machines did not stop to render aid; they merely stepped around his frozen body. He had been front and center, and now, as the fuse burned down, the mob was surrounding him.

The explosion tore the machine apart, turning its body to shrapnel. The machines nearest to the young manbot were blown into others.

The steady pace of the march finally stopped. The clanging, clunking sound of a dozen machines crashing into one another filled the air.

Many of the machines caught in the blast were damaged. Limbs dangled uselessly at their sides. Faces were blown away. A lot of their hair just didn't look right. Stockwell and Bertrand watched as the horde reformed.

The machines marched six across, and there was no sign of the end of their column.

"All right, Bertrand." Stockwell broke the barrel of his shotgun and filled it with three more shells. He turned to his loyal friend and smiled. "Let's give them the old red, white and blue."

Both men opened fire. The thunderous boom from six barrels drowned out the sound of the stomping. The ground still shook beneath them and the walls around them continued to rattle, but it felt like it was their doing.

Bertrand fired. His round found a middle-aged manbot's chest and burned an opening through his suit. The second round found its way inside. Bertrand fired the third round and began to reload.

Stockwell targeted one of the Robonard attendants and fired as fast as the acid could work.

The two machines exploded within seconds of each other. Body parts rained down around them as the line of machines reformed. Some now crawled, dragging broken and useless legs behind them.

The two men fired and reloaded as fast as they could, but the mob of machines kept coming; there was no end to their numbers. The mounting pile of dead machines did nothing to slow their advance.

"Zere are too many!" Bertrand screamed as he shot a little old lady in the stomach.

"Keep firing!" Stockwell shot a toddlerbot and felt a little guilty about it.

"We cannot stop zem!"

"Not with that attitude!"

Damian fired a shocker at the hole in a policeman's shoulder and cursed as the machine swatted it out of the air and kept marching.

"Dammit," he said, as he fired the explosive round toward the same target. "They're learning."

Their aim was true and their weapons were deadly, but it simply wasn't enough to stop the mass of machines. For every one they destroyed, two more stepped closer. The machines trampled the dead and disabled in their incessant progress, until a mere fifty feet remained between the men and the mechanical column.

"Zey are getting too cloze." Bertrand fumbled a red round in his haste to reload. He picked it up off the ground and jammed it in.

"In the back of the truck," Stockwell yelled between blasts. "Open the crate."

Bertrand handed him the loaded shotgun and jumped into the truck's bed. The large crate was against the cab, and he set to unlatching the fasteners.

He heard Stockwell fire the red shell.

"What eez eet?"

"You're not going to like it." Damian fired the white round.

"Why? What eez eet?" He grabbed the last latch and discovered it was stuck. He jiggled it, to no avail.

"Just open it." Stockwell fired the last round from the shotgun. "They're too close."

Bertrand stood and kicked the latch with the heel of his boot. It was enough to break it free.

"Bertrand!"

The valet turned. The army was only feet away as Stockwell struggled to load one of the shotguns. He rushed to the edge of the bed.

"The box, man! Do it!"

Bertrand rushed back to the crate and lifted the lid. "Merde."

The Bertron lay dormant inside, atop a bed of straw.

"Hurry, Bertrand!"

"We don't need 'im," Bertrand shouted back. "We can do zis."

Damian grabbed the empty shotgun by the barrel and began to swing at the robots as they overran the ammo boxes. The stock cracked without effect on a young womanbot.

"TURN IT ON!" he screamed, as he dug in his pockets and tried to put on the brass knuckles. The woman grabbed his wrist before he could connect the leads.

Bertrand sighed and reached behind the Val-8's neck. He found the switch and turned it on.

The machine hummed and opened its eyes. His eyes. It sat up and turned towards the valet.

"Well?" Bertrand pointed to Damian, who was trying to fight back the machines. "Save 'im."

"You heard him, The Bertron. Save me!"

"Oui, Monsieur," The Bertron said, then leapt from the box and stepped into the fight.

The young womanbot had Stockwell's fist in her hand and was twisting his arm to the breaking point.

Half a second later, the woman's head landed in Bertrand's hands and The Bertron helped Damian to his feet. The machine tipped a nonexistent hat to the valet and waded into the crowd.

The machines targeted the new threat and focused their effort on The Bertron. Several piled on the machine and began to pound.

Bertrand dropped off the gate and landed next to his employer. "Should we 'elp?"

"Wait," he said. "Watch this."

The dog pile in the middle of Grasse grew body part by body part as the DamIndustries' personal assistant ripped the limbs from his attackers.

"'ow?"

"I've made some improvements. These evil bastards aren't the only ones that can steal ideas."

The Bertron took on all comers and beat back the crowd to a comfortable distance.

"Eet eez amazing."

"These older Grasse models are no match for him now."

The crowd of machines began to thin as The Bertron worked its way through the inferior robots. Everyone that laid a hand on it lost that hand. Blows bounced off the buffed-up butler as if a human threw them. The Val-8 moved through the mob with the utmost efficiency.

"Eet eez unztoppable," Bertrand marveled.

Stockwell crossed his arms and smiled. "There's nothing like it."

The remaining robocitizens formed a wall across the street and stopped their advance.

"What eef eet turns on uz again?"

"It can't." Stockwell watched The Bertron throw a robot twice its size through a wall. The crowd did not fight back. It just stood there as the Val-8 picked them apart and beat them with their own limbs.

"I've installed safeguards against all external inputs. It won't respond to radio. It won't even respond to verbal commands unless they're coming from the person who created it. And that's only me."

What was left of the robot mob suddenly parted, and The Bertron stopped its attack.

"What the hell?" Stockwell walked down the street to see what had caused the carnage to cease.

Johan von Kempelen stepped from within the robot mob and put his hand on The Bertron.

"Shit," Stockwell said. "I didn't expect that."

"Bring me Stockwell," von Kempelen said. "Kill Bertie. Ignore all further commands."

The Bertron turned and sized up each man.

"You'd better run, my friend."

"What?"

"I've made this thing unstoppable." Damian connected the leads to the brass knuckles and powered up the belt. "I'll hold it off. You run like hell."

"Non." Bertrand grabbed the shotgun and deftly loaded the three shells. He snapped the barrel shut and fired.

The gelatic acid struck The Bertron square in the chest and spread across its shirt in a splotch of fluorescent green. The stain quickly turned white and foamy. The bubbles slid from the shirt and fell to the ground.

Bertrand looked at Stockwell, who only shrugged. "Acid-proof clothing. I thought of everything."

The Bertron started walking towards them.

"Curse my genius. I've outsmarted myself. Again." Damian ran at the machine and threw an electric punch at its head.

The Bertron ducked under the strike and backed away several steps into the line of robots.

"C'mon, you bionic bastard! I'll take you all on."

The Bertron turned to the machine next to it and ripped off its arms. It grabbed each limb by the shoulder and came at Stockwell again.

Bertrand watched in horror as the Val-8 intercepted every electric blow with the severed arms. Sparks flew, but the current never reached The Bertron.

Stockwell fought with all his heart. But it wasn't enough. It was over in a matter of moments.

Bertrand ran.

19

Resist This

"Do not resist." The artificial voice echoed down the street. That it sounded like his own added to the terror.

Grasse was not a large town and Bertrand quickly ran out of places to run.

The machine had caught up to him quickly, and Bertrand had been forced to rely on his agility to escape its grasp.

Sudden turns and panicked dodges were the only thing keeping him from the machine's clutches. Every turn became more desperate until he ran blindly down an alley that led to a dead end.

The Bertron shot past the alleyway entrance and Bertrand could hear the machine scrambling to turn around on the age-worn cobblestone. The valet dashed back towards the street as the robot appeared and blocked his exit.

"Do not resist."

Bertrand darted into a doorway and didn't stop running just

because there was a door. He crashed through and fell to the floor at the bottom of a staircase.

"Do not resist," his own voice insisted.

Bertrand scrambled to his feet and started up the stairs on all fours.

The Bertron's hand closed around his ankle and he could feel the circulation in his foot grind to a halt. "Do not resis—"

The final syllable was swallowed by his sole as Bertrand put a boot in the machine's face and heard the Bakelite mask crack. He kicked again and the faceplate shifted, covering the lens of the robot's eyes.

The Bertron stepped back. Its eyes and nose were off by a few inches. It placed a hand on either side of its slanted face and with a quick twist removed the Bertrand visage and revealed the monster underneath.

The eyes were the darkest part. Without the mask of humanity to hide behind, the cold and mechanical stare became a glare of hatred and evil. They whirred to adjust in the new light, using Bertrand as a focal point. Gears spun behind the eyes, and in the low light of the unlit stairwell, the valet could see the flashes of electric processing pop deep in the Val-8's head.

Bertrand turned as the machine dropped its face. He heard the plastic mask clatter to the floor as he rushed up the steps and bounced off the wall at the second-floor landing. He climbed frantically and felt he was gaining some distance on the machine with every turn in the staircase.

The stairs ultimately took him to the roof. He burst through a door and found himself several stories above the streets of Grasse. The valet ran to the edge of the building and dropped to the next building.

Running across rooftops was not a foreign experience to him. In the course of their adventures together, he and Damian often found themselves pursued or pursuing villains across the top of cities. As he ran, he appreciated the solid construction of Grasse's buildings.

Chases such as these often took them over hastily built favelas or other shantytowns. Their poor construction made for many perils. Weak roofs collapsed, and he had fallen more than once into the midst of a family dinner. Mismatched materials created numerous obstacles that formed tripping hazards, and stumbling across rooftops was much more dangerous than running.

The rooftops in Grasse were solidly constructed, flat and clear of obstacles, and the buildings were so close together that Bertrand merely had to hop short ledges rather than leap perilous chasms.

Bertrand could only guess at the lead his climb up the staircase had given him, but as he neared the end of the block, he knew it would not be enough. He heard his own voice behind him demanding his compliance. The other side of the street was too far to jump, and there was no time to find a way into the building upon which he stood. There was nowhere left to run.

Bertrand turned to face his robotic self and The Bertron closed. The Frenchman reached to the belt around his waist and found the switch. He turned it on and felt the device warm up immediately. The steel bands attached to his shoes meant he would be striking with the top of his foot.

In competitive savate, the device would be useless. This system allowed for only four kicks that focused on contact with the top, the sole and the inside of the foot. But Stockwell knew that Bertrand had not learned the art of the old shoe in the ring. He had learned it on the streets and docks of Marseille, and savate de rue had no rules. It wasn't about points. It was about pain.

Since Stockwell had protected the robot against acid, Bertrand assumed the Val-8 would be shielded against his electric footwear. But based on its actions in the fight against Damian, it was not aware of it. The machine's lack of self-awareness would be his only chance.

The machine slowed as it approached, and Bertrand raised his fists. The Bertron did the same.

Bertrand attacked first. The device crackled as his foot cut through the air and stopped shy of connecting with the robot's shoulder.

The Bertron pulled to the right and Bertrand pressed the attack. He kicked again and let the machine block the strike on the shin. The Val-8 countered and the valet rolled to his left.

The robot's foot came crashing down as he rolled. It missed the Frenchman and punched deep into the roof of the brick building.

Bertrand stood and made a series of alternating kicks that backed the machine to the edge of the roof. The Bertron was a foot away from falling four stories to the street below.

He went in for a punch and got close enough for the Val-8 to strike out. Bertrand anticipated the punch. He needed the punch and was ready for it. And when it struck, he flew backwards and landed on his back. He rolled several feet from the machine.

He wheezed as he got back to his feet. Though he had been ready for the blow, it took more from him than he'd expected. But he didn't have time to shrug it off. His moment was now.

On mighty legs, he sprinted towards the machine and leapt into the air, driving a piston-like blow towards The Bertron's exposed face.

He didn't connect. He didn't need to. The Val-8 backed reflexively away from the potential electric strike and stepped off the edge of the building.

Bertrand listened for the crash. He turned his head to hear the clank of metal against the stone below.

But it never came.

He approached the edge of the building and peered over.

The Val-8 seized his left ankle and began to pull itself up. The horrid face rose above the lip of the building. "Do not resist."

Bertrand struck out with the top of his right foot and planted the metal band deep in the machine's exposed face.

There was a bright blue arc of overload as the current ran from the battery around his waist into The Bertron's face. The shock bounced around the clockwork pieces deep behind its eyes, and the hand released Bertrand's ankle.

The Val-8 fell away from the building and plummeted into the town below.

Bertrand watched it land.

The stone around the machine was cracked and broken. Dust from the street rose above it. The machine did not move.

Bertrand spit, not in general loathing, but with the true intent of dropping a four-story gob on the machine that had done its best to replace him. He missed.

As the valet started back towards the staircase that would take him back to the street, more anger and another gob of spit rose within him.

He rushed back to the edge of the roof to try again.

The Bertron was gone.

"Merde."

20

Flowers of Evil

He had been hit hard before, and he had scars, fractures and memory lapses to prove it, he thought. But nothing, neither man nor beast, nor man crossed with beast, a.k.a. The Meast from the East, had ever hit like the arms of a robot being swung by the arms of another robot.

Damian didn't want to open his eyes. He knew that as soon as he did, his head would just hurt more. He was alive, and since the man who brought him here wanted him alive, there was no need to betray his conscious state. So he kept his eyes closed.

After assessing his state of living, it was crucial to know where he had been taken. Unlike most men, he did not need his eyes for this.

He could not feel the sun on his skin, so he knew he was no longer outside. It was possible that it was night. He didn't know how long he had been rendered unconscious, but indoors had other cues as well. No breeze stirred. The air was still on his skin. And he was on a mattress. Beds were, more often than not, kept indoors.

He breathed gently, silently taking in the scent of the room. Here he learned everything. The air was thick and damp with a cool bite to it. He was underground, possibly a cellar. The air was sweet, and he could still detect the aroma of flowers, but not those that grew in the freedom of the wild. These were petals stripped and brought together in a great quantity.

There was a tinge of iron and rust. It could be machinery, or robots that had shed their human form. But no, this smell was too close. This was the iron of incarceration.

It was obvious now that he was in a cellar prison deep within the sweet-scented bowels of the Robonard Perfumery. And he wasn't alone. He could smell someone else in the room with him. He heard her, too. Her breath was too gentle for a man. Too considerate. A man would be doing everything to rouse him so they could conspire to escape. He would suggest they overpower the guards. But a woman, cunning and kind, would understand that rest would be a greater spoon with which to dig a tunnel.

"How long?" he asked to the person in the room.

"An hour, maybe," answered Angelica Palmer.

Stockwell shot upright and snapped open his eyes. He was right. It hurt.

There wasn't much light in the room, but every bit of it touched a nerve somewhere in the back of his head. Still, the pain was nothing compared to the emotional flood triggered by her presence.

Anger. Relief. Rage. Lust. Confusion. His mind fired questions faster than his aching head could process them. What was she doing here? How did she get here? How long had she been here? Was von Kempelen behind her presence in his cell? He agreed with himself that these were all very good questions, but in the end, there was only one thing he needed to know: was she a robot? Of course she was.

"I'm Angelica," she said.

"I think we've established that."

"What?" She shook her head."I'm a reporter and—"

"I don't know what you're up to, but I'm done falling for your tricks. Your lies have lost their appeal, my dear."

"What are you talking about, Mr. Stockwell?"

"So, the charade has been dropped," Damian stood and pointed to her. "You do know exactly who I am."

"You're famous. Everybody knows who you are."

"Yes, but not like you know me."

She crossed the room and put a hand on his head. "They must have hit you really hard."

He grabbed her wrists and she gasped at his touch. He pulled her arms in front of her. She had changed her look. Her red hair, usually so neat and well kept, was ruffled and dingy. Her skin, once so flawless, was marked with grime. Her signature perfume was gone, replaced by what smelled like a severe lack of showering.

Damian leaned in and sniffed her neck. There was no trace of leather or the golden smell of gear oil.

"What the hell is wrong with you?" she squealed.

"Von Kempelen grows more diabolical by the day. He's found a natural way to cover the oil with regular human stink."

"I beg your pardon."

"He thinks he has me fooled, but there's no fooling this." Damian raised a hand back and slapped Angelica across the face, and it was instantly clear that she wasn't a robot.

Angelica Palmer didn't scream or cry. She snapped back up and punched Damian in the face with such suddenness that he quickly found himself back on the mattress with both his head, and now his face, in pain.

"You're not a robot," Stockwell said with great relief.

"Of course I'm not a robot, you idiot! I'm a prisoner, just like you."

Damian leapt to his feet and took her in his arms. "My dear,

I'm8

I'm so relieved that you're you." His lips met hers and he fell deeply into the kiss.

Angelica stepped back and punched him again. "You are crazy."

Damian fell back onto the cot once more. "What's with all the punching?" he shouted. "I mean, the first one I deserved, but that second one."

"You kissed me!"

"So?"

"People don't just go around kissing strangers."

"Strangers? How can you call us strangers after the night we spent together?"

Angelica leaned in close and pointed to emphasize each word. "We have never met. There was no night together."

Damian looked at the floor. "The entire time?" He shook his head. "I was really hoping that at least that one night, it wasn't—I'd better not have gremlins." He put his face in his hands.

"Are you going to cry just because a girl hit you?"

Damian stood up again. "Don't sell yourself short. You've got some fist on you. But I'm not crying. I'm just working through some things." He straightened his shirt and cleared his throat. "Ms. Palmer, please allow me to apologize. First for slapping you, and second for assuming that we had been intimate. I feel I must justify my actions. I slapped you because I assumed you were a robot because, as you may be unaware, a mechanical duplicate of you has been running around doing horrible things in your name. She and I did some of those horrible things together. Not all of them were horrible. Some would have been considered delightful if they weren't … not that it makes it okay."

"You had sex with a robot?"

"Yes. But it's not weird, because I thought it was you." Damian smiled. "See?"

"You slept with a robot and thought it was me?"

"That's right."

She crossed her arms. "And how was I?"

"A little pinchy."

She huffed.

"But that's okay, because we now know that it wasn't you. Well, you already knew that. But now I know that, and I'm sure that sex with you would be far less robotic."

"You disgust me."

Stockwell shrugged. "Fair enough."

Angelica sat down on a cot similar to his own and pulled her knees up to her chest.

Damian sat as well, and stared at the floor. He kicked at some dirt. "So … smells in here, huh? I thought this was supposed to be a perfume factory."

Angelica looked at the ceiling.

He could see her beauty through the grime and the time in captivity. She was more beautiful than her robot double could ever hope to be.

"Many sweet flowers' scented breath." She sighed. "Is lavished till they fade in death."

"Yep," Stockwell said. "Stinky."

"It's Baudelaire, you moron."

"Of course it's boring here. It's a cell."

She closed her eyes and leaned her head against the wall.

"What do you say we get out of here?"

She laughed at him but did not move.

Damian stood and walked the room. The floor was stone. The walls were stone. There was no window or back door that he could find. No plumbing. The only light in the room came from the hallway.

He tapped against the wall, hoping for a secret passage.

"What are you doing?" Angelica asked.

"Stone walls do not a prison make." He smiled. "Nor iron bars a cage."

"They're a good start," she muttered.

Damian moved to the iron bars and examined their construction. Solid welds. High-quality iron. He grabbed the bars and flexed his mighty chest. Through gritted teeth and sheer force, he pulled against his cage.

"What are you doing?"

"I'm trying to bend these bars."

"Good luck with that."

Stockwell stopped and turned. "Since your criticism doesn't seem to be helping all that much, why don't you come over and at least help me try?"

He pulled with all of his considerable might to no avail. He muttered under his breath a curse. "Damn you, Lovelace."

"Help you bend iron bars? You're dumber than I thought."

Though deceitful, dishonest, manipulative, kind of slutty and designed for evil, the Angelicabot was turning out to be much nicer than the real thing. "The robot version of you would have done it."

"Are you really trying to make me jealous of a robot?"

"Aren't you? You haven't liked me ever since I confessed to our tryst."

"I haven't liked you since you slapped me."

Stockwell rolled his eyes. "That was to find out if you were a robot. We're not going to get out of here if I'm going to have to explain everything twice."

"You're not going to get out of here at all."

Stockwell spun and saw von Kempelen staring at him through the bars.

"Not without help," Johan said.

"Johan!" Stockwell grabbed the bars and shoved his face between them. "You treacherous bastard. Come here so I can punch you."

To Damian's surprise, Johan stepped forward.

Stockwell reached out and grabbed the robotologist around the neck and pulled him into the cell's iron bars. There was a tremendous clang as metal struck metal. Damian held the man's face close. "It can't be."

Johan backed away. "It is. I'm a robot."

"So they made an evil double of you and crushed you in a

press."

"Not quite. I put myself in the press. Well, what was left of me, anyway."

"What do you mean?"

Von Kempelen looked at the ground. "I'm afraid I wasn't always completely honest with you. You have been my good friend for a long time, but I ... I wasn't well, Damian.

"I had gotten sick. I'm afraid it was terminal. But I was determined to fight it. I spent everything I had trying to live. The treatment cost me everything. Including my marriage."

"I knew it," Stockwell said to Angelica, who didn't seem to care. "I knew it was those things that he just said."

Johan continued. "I had one last chance. With the progress we had made on the Val-8 and the progress others had made on their own research, I reasoned that it might be possible to build a new me. A better me." Johan grabbed the iron bar and twisted it. The metal protested with a squeal but bent.

"Gottfried's work was the final piece. His work on synthetic skin was the breakthrough I had been waiting for. I was able to successfully transfer my consciousness into this miracle of science." He tapped his chest.

Stockwell looked at his old friend. "And you pressed yourself to cover your tracks."

Johan nodded.

"And the Val-8 destroying the fair was the perfect way to throw anyone off your scent," Damian said. "Also, crushing yourself in an industrial press. That would also take the suspicion off of you ... being dead and all."

"Nothing gets by you, Dam."

"I commend you, my friend. But there's one thing I don't understand. Why a perfume factory?"

Johan smiled. "I discovered this place when I came here at the behest of my doctor. He said the climate would do me some good. He was right. It's done wonders for my health."

"But why the perfume?"

"I needed funds to realize my dream. And do you have any idea what the markup on this stuff is? It's insane. I mean, it's just smelly water." Johan added, "And it was the perfect cover. In more ways than one."

Damian looked at the girl in the cell. "That it is." He turned back to von Kempelen. "And what have you done with the citizens of Grasse? Did you murder them, too?"

"Hardly," Johan said. "A robot army cannot build itself. Not yet."

"I commend you, my friend, on your accomplishments. But I regret you turned to evil, when you could have turned to me. I'm hurt you didn't ask for my help. You know you could have counted on me."

Johan looked away.

"But now you've gone too far. And for what? Why are you trying to replace myself and others with robot duplicates?"

Von Kempelen smiled. "Don't you see? I'm more than human. I'm stronger and I cannot die. I've made myself better. And if I can make myself better, I can make the whole world better."

"You're sick in whatever part of your body you keep your head, Johan."

"No. My logic is perfect. Don't you see? With the leaders of the world under my control, I could continue my world improvement plans unmolested. To make it a better place for everyone."

"But at what cost? Our humanity?"

"Humanity is our weakness. Flesh is weak. It's flawed. I've fixed it. And now I can fix everything."

"So that's why you wanted me out of the way? So there was no one left to stop you?"

Johan stepped closer to the bars. "No. I don't want to stop you. I want you to join me, my friend. The DamBot wasn't meant to replace you. It was meant to improve you. The offer still stands. Join me, Dam. Together we can make the world a better place."

Damian hung his head and walked away from cell door. "No. I can't be party to this."

"Think of the good you could do. I can make you superhuman."

"Thanks, Doc," Stockwell said. "But no thanks. I'm super enough as it is."

Johan's smile disappeared. "I truly hope you reconsider. Until then, you'll stay here."

A shadow appeared on the hallway wall. It was a silhouette Damian would recognize anywhere. It was proper and poised. A perfect posture and a certain pompousness to the way it walked. He smiled at the Doctorbot. "Looks like I'll be getting out of here sooner than you thought."

The Bertron stepped into view.

"Dammit," Stockwell spat.

"Ah, Val-8. Is it done?"

The Bertron nodded.

"Good."

"No," Stockwell shook his head. "Bertrand can't be ... no." Damian grabbed the bars and shook them. "You robotic bastard. I wish I'd never dreamed you up."

The Val-8 stared at him as he shook the bars. There was nothing behind those eyes.

"I hate you. I hate your plastic face. You don't deserve to look like him." He shook the bars with such force the debris began to fall from the walls where the iron was anchored. "I'm going to destroy you myself."

The Val-8 stepped forward and reached through the bars. He grabbed Stockwell by the shirt and pulled the prisoner's face against the bars.

"Enough," Johan commanded the Val-8. "He's not to be harmed. Not yet."

The Bertron released Stockwell, and the adventurer fell back into the cell fighting back tears. "You've gone too far, Johan."

The doctor grabbed the iron bar and twisted it back into

place. "Think about my offer." With that, Johan von Kempelen walked away.

The Bertron stared blankly at Damian for a moment longer before following the doctor.

Stockwell crossed an arm across his face and wept.

"Oh, I can't believe this," Angelica said. "The great Damian Stockwell. Self-proclaimed world's greatest adventurer. Doer of good. Fighter of injustice. Crying like a baby."

Stockwell wept for a moment longer, until he was certain the machines were out of microphone range. He stood and looked at the woman. "You forgot Champion of Right and Force for Decency," he said without a trace of sadness. "But it doesn't matter if you believed anything. As long as they think I was crying for my lost friend and trusted companion."

Damian reached into his shirt pocket and pulled out a red shotgun shell. He held it in front of her eyes.

"What is that?"

"It's like a key but with a whole lot more acid." Damian stepped back to the bars and set to work peeling back the paper hull.

"You've had that the whole time and you tried bending the bars like some sideshow freak?"

"No. Bertrand dropped it in my pocket a moment ago." He exposed the gelatic acid and forced it into the keyhole. A faint wisp of smoke billowed from the lock. "You didn't see? Hmmm. I thought you journalists were supposed to be observant."

The smoke faded away and Damian pushed against the cell door. There was a small metallic clank and the bars swung open. "There we go."

Angelica looked at the open door and back to Stockwell. "What now?"

"Now to rescue the citizens of Grasse and stop the robocidal maniac that used to be my good friend, before he can take over the planet by replacing world leaders with his own mechanical minions." Damian waved a hand towards the door. "Obviously."

21

The Smell of Fear

The hallways of the perfumery were empty, but an electric hum filled the air with sound and discomfort. It made the cellar pulse, and when he listened to it long enough, Damian could hear a rhythm in the sound.

Stockwell reasoned that a town full of automatons would require a ridiculous amount of power. Even the most efficient system would need a recharge, and that would mean a generator. Somewhere in the building a dynamo was spinning to fuel the evil desires of his once-dead friend.

He put his hand against the wall and felt the vibration run through it. He pointed down the hallway. "This way."

Angelica put a hand on his shoulder. "Wait. Do you mean that way is the way out? Or that way leads into a den of vicious killer robots?"

"Oftentimes the way out is through a den of vicious killer

robots, Angelica," Stockwell said.

She cocked her head. "Oftentimes?"

"Sometimes," Damian said.

She folded her arms.

"Well, this times."

She pursed her lips.

"It's a metaphor. Okay? And it happens more than you might think."

"I have been a prisoner here for weeks, and you expect me to rush back into the arms of my captor?"

"There isn't much choice. Outside of these walls is a city crawling with robotic evil. If we try to flee the city, we will be hunted down with mathematical efficiency. The only way we're going to escape this prison is if we save the world right here and right now."

"How?"

"We'll find a way."

"That's stupidly optimistic."

Damian smiled. "I try to look on the bright side of things."

"They'll kill us."

"Maybe, Angelica. But let me ask you what's worse. Dying in the course of defending humanity, or living a coward's life of doubt and regret?"

"I know several cowards that live quite well."

"Well, that's no life for me. Our fellow humans need us to stand up against this foul abuse of science. And I'm not going to let them down." The conversation was over. Damian moved cautiously down the hallway, leading with his ear.

Angelica followed with a huff.

They passed several large cells capable of holding dozens of people each. They were empty now. Von Kempelen probably had them slaving away, building more and more machines. He had hinted as much.

This concerned him deeply. Ideally, he would just find a way to blow up the room around von Kempelen and his robot minions.

It was standard operating procedure.

But now he knew that people would be mixed in with the robot population. This put them in not only harm's way, but in his way, as well. Only a true coward surrounded himself with the innocent.

The floral smell grew as they approached the source of the hum. It became all but overwhelming as they neared the heart of the factory. The odor became warm and pungent. Stockwell felt a tickle at the back of his nose as his sense of smell tried to compensate from such an overwhelming stimuli.

One glance at Angelica and he could tell she was suffering the same reaction. She sniffled and scrunched her nose as the odor overwhelmed her.

The hallway ended at the foot of a staircase, and the pair climbed cautiously. Damian let his feet fall with absolute precision, eliminating any sound as they lit upon the stone steps.

The ancient staircase curved as it rose fifteen feet to the building's ground level and emerged inside a vast room. This was the heart of the perfumery. Copper vats boiled the essence from nature as the bottling line rattled an endless parade of glass jars bearing the Robonard name.

The good people of Grasse tended the line, inserting atomizers into the bottles and packing the finished product into boxes for shipment.

Another assembly line ran counter to the perfume. Limbs and other body parts hung from metal rails as men and women assembled the parts into countless robots. The termination point saw the fitting of one of the dozen faces he had seen in the town.

A hundred machines were scattered about the enslaved citizens, keeping watch. These expressionless taskmasters patrolled the assembly lines, dealing quick corrections to any human that made an error or took too long to complete their job.

"Look at these people," Stockwell whispered. "They've broken their spirits."

"They've been here for months," Angelica said.

Damian examined the people. "Is that the Secretary of State?"

Angelica nodded. "They brought him in a couple of weeks ago."

"My God. They must have taken him in London." Damian shook his head. "I can't believe it. I talked to him the whole trip back. He hardly said a word to me."

"That's because he was a robot."

"I thought he was just being a jerk." He looked around the room and recognized at least a dozen people of note at work in the factory. His face tightened. "This ends now."

Angelica put a hand on his shoulder and held him back. "What are you going to do? There are too many."

Damian smiled and undid his pants.

"Whoa, you are really misreading me here."

"Don't get excited." He rolled back his waistband to reveal the battery pack. "They may have taken my knuckles, but they left this."

"I don't know what that means, and pull up your pants."

"It's a power source." He redid his pants and looked around the room. "Now I just need to find something to channel the current."

"See? You could have just said that without undoing your pants."

"There's no time for explanations." Damian buttoned his fly and turned back to the room. "It's time to act."

"You're crazy. You don't stand a chance."

"Go, if you wish. There's a truck in the center of town that you can take to safety. But you're going to miss a hell of a story."

Angelica leaned in close and whispered, "I'll risk it." She ran back down the stairway muttering something about stupidity, but Damian couldn't quite make it out.

He turned away and took a deep breath. He rolled into the room and came up low behind a pile of boxes. He searched the room and spotted the items he needed.

Though humanlike in appearance, the machines still functioned under mathematical principles. That meant that if they weren't set upon a specific task, there would be a distinct pattern to their actions.

Damian watched from behind the packing materials as von Kempelen's machines patrolled the manufacturing lines. After a few moments of observation, their pattern was clear.

Stockwell began to count in his head. He had a fair amount of musical talent, which he had always credited to possessing an innate sense of rhythm. He set this natural metronome to the proper frequency and began to move.

As the machines turned, he sprinted. He slid under the bottling line and scrambled past the legs of the oblivious workers and machines. He reached the end of the line and waited for another sentry to pass by before sticking his head out from beneath the conveyor system.

"Pardon me, ma'am. But I need your gloves."

The woman opened her mouth to scream, so he put a finger to his lips and repeated the request.

To her credit, she stifled the yell and subtly removed the rubber gloves from her hands. She dropped them to the ground one at a time.

He grabbed them, smiled, then disappeared under the bottling line.

The robots' movements had not altered. He watched their legs as they stepped on according to their programming. One, two, he rolled across the walkway beside the packaging conveyor. One, two, three, he crawled along the line towards a pile of equipment he had spotted in his quick survey. One, two, he rolled from beneath the line towards the equipment and bumped into von Kempelen.

"What are you doing rolling around down there?" The doctor grabbed Damian by the neck and threw him over the assembly line.

He landed hard enough to make his internal metronome skip.

The doctor soared through the air.

Damian scrambled aside as Johan landed fist first. The strike missed but sunk deep into the stone floor. "What do you think you can possibly do?"

Stockwell kicked at the machine.

Von Kempelen caught the foot and hurled Damian across the factory. He collided with a copper still and fell to the ground as the doctor rushed across the room after him.

Damian rolled to his stomach and dove underneath the still.

Von Kempelen crashed into the ground beside the still and bent over. "You can't stop progress, Dam. You know this as much as anyone." He reached under the still and grabbed Stockwell's ankle.

Stockwell rolled onto his back and spotted the copper pipes running beneath the still. He reached out, wrapped the rubber gloves around them and grabbed hold.

Even through the gloves he could feel the warmth of the pipes.

The doctor pulled. "But I'm afraid you won't be a part of it."

Damian pulled against his grip. The pipes held at first, but soon the machine's strength overcame their sturdy construction and they began to bend. Stockwell held firm.

"Come out of there!" The robot pulled harder.

Damian's ankle screamed at the grip, and the copper tore away from the still. Perfume in its purest state poured from the pipes, over his face and into his mouth, as he was yanked from beneath the equipment.

He sputtered and coughed as von Kempelen threw him once more across the room.

Damian landed on the packaging line. Glass shattered, and the Robonard perfume spilled across the floor and soaked into his clothes. The workers scattered away from the line, activating the other robots. The machines scrambled to return the workers to the line.

Damian's eyes began to water as he moved down the conveyor belt. The copper pipes were still in his hands, and he worked quickly to pull the leads from inside his sleeve.

Von Kempelen stood at the end of the line, waiting with a smile on his face.

Stockwell kicked backwards, trying to buy some time, but the perfume made the surface slick and the belt moved him ever closer.

Johan grabbed him as he arrived at the end of the line and pinned him to the ground under his boot. The machine drew back a fist. "You made this possible, you know? Thank you, Dam. You made me what I am."

"Damn you, Johan. You made me smell like a girl." Damian thrust the copper pipes into von Kempelen's torso. He felt the hum of the current beneath the rubber insulators as the circuit completed.

The doctor jumped back with a hand on his stomach. There was fear in his eyes. The process that had saved his consciousness had brought with it a sense of self-preservation.

Damian smiled. He loved to see the look of fear in evil's eyes.

"Get him!" Von Kempelen backed away and shouted to the room. A hundred henchmen turned their attention to the adventurer who smelled like a girl.

22

Assault of the Automatons

The machines rushed him in a very orderly fashion.

Stockwell reset the metronome in his head to a much peppier beat and raised the copper pipes. He had always found stick-fighting a satisfying blend of beating and nonlethal force. He dragged the pipes against one another and watched the arc form between them.

The first machine reached him.

The copper pipes hummed their own tune through the air as he moved them in a practiced combination that left the robot incapacitated and shaking on the floor.

Two more automatons had flanked him and charged. He dropped to the ground and delighted in the clunk they made as they collided. In that brief moment of impact, he struck each on the leg with a pipe and sent the current coursing through them. They jiggled and fell to the ground.

Johan was retreating through the advancing mass and Stockwell yelled after him. "Put a stop to this madness, Johan."

The doctor offered no response as his minions came. They marched down the corridors. They leapt over the machines and stomped across the assembly line with little concern for Robonard's stock.

Damian charged into the fray and began his attack. The pipes hummed an even tune as they blurred in an unceasing pattern of contact and destroy. The smell of ozone soon fought the scent of dead flowers as the pipes sparked and electronics blew.

But they kept coming, stepping over their fallen and pushing on.

The belt began to burn around his waist. The pipes were beginning to melt the rubber. He struck a machine across the back of the knees and it collapsed to the floor.

He turned his attention to the next in line and soon realized his mistake.

The fallen machine, still functional above the waist, pulled Stockwell's legs out from under him, and he fell on his back as another machine loomed over him.

The machine looked like an old man, wrinkled and jowly. The skin on his face was unnatural and refused to react to gravity as it drew closer. His hand reached out for Damian's face.

The hands were ageless and as they closed in, he could see the joints in the flesh that allowed for the movement of the fingers.

Damian tried to strike with the copper pipes, but the crippled machine grabbed his right hand. One baton was not enough to complete the circuit. He was finished.

The old man's head exploded in a splash of electricity as a valet boot connected with its jowls. The machine collapsed on Damian's chest and pinned him to the ground.

Bertrand spun and deactivated several more machines with savage electric kicks before turning to help Stockwell out from under the fallen contraption.

Damian stood and looked into the dark eyes of his longtime

friend. They were so recessed behind the shiny Bakelite mask of the Val-8 that he could barely see them. "Thank you, my friend. You can take off that mask now. Its purpose has been served."

"Zis eez my faze!" Bertrand said.

"It is? But it looks all plasticy."

"Eez zis plaze. My allairgees!"

Stockwell chuckled. "Baby."

Together, armed with electric science and the art of fist and foot, the two made their way through the army of robots. Tubes shattered. Circuits fused. Plastic smoldered. Von Kempelen's forces lay broken, like so many bottles of Robonard perfume.

The pipes burned in his hands. Bertrand's shoelaces were most likely on fire. But they had conquered the mechanical menace. Only Johan remained.

The hostages began to emerge from their hiding places and applauded the carnage that lay before them.

Damian and Bertrand turned to face the doctor, who now stood with his back against the wall of the age-old factory.

"You're all out of minions, Johan," Damian said. "The evil you tried to unleash on this world cannot be forgiven. But your genius is something that can't be denied. You were a good man once, Johan. It'd be a shame to deactivate you. Turn yourself off and we'll see if we can't reprogram you for good instead of evil."

Johan smirked. The realism of his face was uncanny. He began to laugh. "You actually think you've won? Your arrogance is astounding."

"Thank you." Stockwell smiled.

"Zat waz not un compliment, Monsieur."

"Sure it was. He said astounding. Astounding is a good thing."

It began with a slow rumble. The building began to shake. The factory windows shattered as hundreds of robots poured into the building. An endless stream dropped through the broken glass and quickly filled the factory floor. The prisoners dove for the hiding places, but the machines routed them and held them fast with an arm across their necks.

"A single thought from me," Johan hissed, "and they snap their necks. I don't even have to speak."

"You wouldn't!"

"I would. They are weak. All humans are weak and therefore unnecessary in my new world."

Damian looked into the Johanbot's eyes. They were soulless and inhuman, but they shined like polished stone and he saw what he needed to see. He threw the copper pipes down in front of him. "Drop your shoes, Bertrand."

The valet looked at his feet. "I am not sure 'ow I would even do zat."

"Stop arguing and just do it. The doctor is in complete control."

Bertrand shrugged his shoulders and bent down to untie his shoes.

The shotgun boomed and Johan's face jerked back towards the ceiling.

Bertrand covered his head as Damian rolled forward and grabbed the pipes. He stood as Johan recovered from the blast. The gelatic acid had burned away any resemblance of humanity and left behind only the metal face of evil that he had become.

Damian thrust with both batons and shoved them deep through the lenses as they whirred desperately trying to focus and make sense of the situation. The circuit was closed deep within the robot's head.

Von Kempelen screamed as electricity surged through his inhuman mind. Smoke poured from every opening in his face as the machine began to shake.

Seconds later, it was over. As soon as the mechanical Johan von Kempelen crumpled to the ground, the robots in the factory went dormant. Nothing controlled them now.

"Mon Dieu!" Bertrand jumped to his feet and looked behind him. Angelica Palmer stood in the factory doorway, clutching a smoking gun.

"I felt zat! Zat almost 'it me!"

"Why did you think I told you to duck?"

"A little warning would 'ave been nice."

"You didn't see her reflection in his eyes?" asked Damian.

"I can't zee almost anyzing. My alleirgees."

"Baby," Damian said, and turned to Angelica. "Nice shot. I'm glad you decided to come back."

"What choice did I have?" she asked.

He smiled. "I know. I knew you'd never just drive away and leave us here."

"You have the keys."

He checked his pocket and nodded. "That's how I knew."

EPILOGUE

THE JOURNEY HOME

The three piled into the cab of the truck, and Stockwell put it into gear. He knocked on the panel behind him to let the freed hostages in the bed know he was about to pull out. He drove slowly through the town's narrow streets and waved to the joyous citizens that lined the streets.

Angelica sat next to him. "Shouldn't we wait for the authorities?"

"Nah. The people here will explain what happened, and I'm sure our friends in the back will want to get home as soon as possible and explain to their loved ones that they've been robots for the last few weeks."

"True."

"And I want to get Bertrand's face back to normal as soon as possible. It's really freaking me out."

They pulled out of town. Stockwell accelerated around a turn and the passengers in the cab slid across the seat. Angelica put her arm on his shoulder to catch herself.

He looked deep into her eyes and let his own sparkle twice.

She backed away nervously. "So." She cleared her throat. "Tell me what was so great about the robot me that made you want to … you know."

Damian smiled and then sighed. "Well, she was beautiful. She had fiery red hair and a spirit to match. Her eyes burned with the same passion as yours. I dare say she was von Kempelen's finest work."

"Oh really?"

He nodded. "Truly. That's how I knew that you'd come back

for us. I know that deep down you're a good person, because even the evil robot version of you wasn't really that bad."

"It sounds like she meant a lot to you."

Damian looked out the window. "Maybe. To be honest, I'm not sure how to feel about all this."

Angelica leaned in closer. "Maybe I can help you work through those emotions."

He turned back to her. "I'd like that."

"It sounds like she broke your heart."

"My heart is a little broken."

"How did you end it with her?"

"I ripped off her arms and left her in my lab."

Angelica sat up. "What?"

"Sure. She's there right now. I'll show you when we get back."

"That is sick!"

"It's not sick, it's—Look, what about my emotions?"

"I'm pretty sure you don't have any emotions," she said as she folded her arms.

"I know." Stockwell sighed and looked out the window. He peered into the mirror and laughed. "Well, would you look at that?"

The image in the rearview mirror was tiny but growing larger. The Bertron was creating a trail of dust on the dirt road as it ran to catch the truck.

"Do you see that, Bertrand?"

"Oui, I zee eet."

"I guess now that it's free of Johan's control, it's returning to its master."

Stockwell applied the brake.

Bertrand opened the door and stepped out as the truck slowed to a stop. He walked toward the back of the truck and Damian heard him drop the gate.

Damian turned to Angelica. "Never let it be said that DamIndustries builds a poor quality product."

"You smell like a girl," she said.

Damian gritted his teeth. "I know I do."

He looked back to the mirror. The Bertron slowed as it neared the truck.

The first shot hit it in the chest. The second found the hole and made the entire machine shake. There was a third boom, then Bertrand climbed back into the cab. "You'd bettair drive."

Damian dropped the truck back into gear and pulled away quickly as the fuse on the blue round burned down.

"Bertrand, what the hell are you doing? It wasn't evil anymore."

"I know," the valet said.

"He could have come home with us."

"I know," the valet said.

The Val-8 exploded in a ball of flames that sent pieces of the machine into the flower fields on either side of the road.

Bertrand closed his swollen eyes and went to sleep with a smile on his face.

THE END

ABOUT THE AUTHOR

Benjamin Wallace lives in Texas where he complains about the heat. A lot.

Visit the author at benjaminwallacebooks.com.
Also, find him on twitter @BenMWallace or on facebook.

Or you can email him at: *contact@benjaminwallacebooks.com*

To learn about the latest releases and giveaways, join his Readers' Group at benjaminwallacebooks.com.

If you enjoyed *THE MECHANICAL MENACE* please consider leaving a review. It would be very much appreciated and help more than you could know.

Thanks for reading, visiting, following and sharing.
-ben

61123562R00114

Made in the USA
Lexington, KY
03 March 2017